J Folsom X
Folsom, Franklin
Sand dune pony

$12.95
SANI ocn813541129
1st Taylor Trad   08/07/2013

The Wilderness Mystery Series

The Diamond Cave Mystery

The Forest Fire Mystery

The Hidden Ruin

The Indian Mummy Mystery

The Jinx of Payrock Canyon

The Mystery at Rustler's Fort

Sand Dune Pony

SAND DUNE PONY

Troy Nesbit

TAYLOR TRADE PUBLISHING
Lanham • New York • Boulder • Toronto • Plymouth, UK

Published by Taylor Trade Publishing
An imprint of The Rowman & Littlefield Publishing Group, Inc.
4501 Forbes Boulevard, Suite 200, Lanham, Maryland 20706
www.rowman.com

10 Thornbury Road, Plymouth PL6 7PP, United Kingdom

Distributed by National Book Network

British Library Cataloguing in Publication Information Available

Library of Congress Cataloging-in-Publication Data Available

ISBN 978-1-58979-811-3 (pbk. : alk. paper)
ISBN 978-1-58979-812-0 (electronic)

♾™ The paper used in this publication meets the minimum
requirements of American National Standard for Information
Sciences—Permanence of Paper for Printed Library Materials,
ANSI/NISO Z39.48-1992.

Printed in the United States of America.

CONTENTS

ILLUSTRATIONS

Crackerjack Had Thrown Slim Again

SAND DUNE PONY

CHAPTER ONE

NO HORSE TO RIDE

Pete sat on the opry-house rail of the corral with every muscle tense. In a minute, Slim would be trying once more to take the kinks out of Crackerjack. Pete's Uncle Lem said that Slim was a "top peeler," which meant that the cowboy was a first-rate bronc buster. But so far, Slim hadn't been able to get anywhere with Crackerjack. Day after day the horse had unloaded him. Pete hoped this time would be different. He wanted Crackerjack turned into a good cow pony—"rough-broke and then topped off," Slim called it. Until that happened, Pete couldn't depend on having a horse to ride.

Pete envied Slim now, as the cowboy tightened the cinch on the saddle. He was sure he could stay on the hurricane deck of a bronc as well as Slim could, although he'd never ridden anything but gentle stable horses back in Chicago. And he'd done plenty of that after school and on Saturdays when he worked as stable boy for his friend Tim Mulligan who kept horses for people to ride in the park.

With Slim in the saddle and the blindfold off the bronc's eyes, Crackerjack gave a few mild crowhops, then suddenly exploded into the air and came down with all four legs stiff. Once, twice, three times, the horse did this pile-driver trick, and Slim's head snapped around like a leaf on the end of a twig. On his fourth leap, Crackerjack turned almost end for end in mid-air.

"He's showing daylight!" Pete yelled, as the bronc heaved Slim up out of the saddle. Slim struggled to regain his balance, but Crackerjack had his number. The horse sunfished twice—throwing first his right shoulder almost to the ground and then his left. That was the end of Slim's ride.

As the cowboy picked himself up out of the dust, Uncle Lem Perkins shook his head. "It's a wonder that hombre has any bones left in his body. Crackerjack has had Slim picking daisies every day for a week now."

"I'd like to try Crackerjack, Uncle Lem," said Pete. "How about giving me a chance tomorrow?"

"I know you can ride, Pete," Uncle Lem said. "But the answer is still no. I just can't take a chance on having any more men from this ranch in the hospital. You know what a run of bad luck there's been around here. I even hate to let Slim fork those ponies in the rough string. I swear I don't know what I'd do if I lost another hand."

Pete knew that his uncle was talking sense.

"Sure," he said. "You're right. I just wish I could be a little more help myself." He meant it, but he knew he couldn't do much except chores around the place until he had a horse to ride and could get a little experience working with the regular cowhands. Still, he wasn't one to give up easily. He had come here to ride and he intended to, one way or another. Last winter in Chicago, when Uncle Lem and Aunt Clara came East to visit, Uncle Lem had promised Pete a summer—and a horse—on his Lazy B-5 Ranch in Colorado. Pete had worked almost every day in the stable and saved every penny in order to pay his bus fare West.

But when he arrived day before yesterday he found that things had gone wrong. In the spring, Uncle Lem's barn had burned down one day while he was out on the range, destroying his truck and tractor. In order to make the payments on new equipment and the fine new barn, Uncle Lem had sold all except two of his good cow horses. His three cowhands were riding half-broken animals while they did their summer work on the range. And Slim was staying around now, training a new string of horses to take the place of the ones Uncle Lem had sold, getting them in shape for the fall roundup.

But that wasn't the worst of it. Uncle Lem had

kept Rocket, a spirited but well-broken horse, for Pete to ride during the summer. Then, the day before Pete arrived, all kinds of trouble started. Rocket broke his leg and had to be shot. That left only the broncs and Uncle Lem's own horse, Bridger. Then one of the cowboys got appendicitis and yesterday Uncle Lem had driven him to the hospital in Alamosa.

Pete had had a chance to ride Bridger his first day on the ranch. But from now on, he knew, such chances would be scarce until Slim had really topped off Crackerjack or one of the other rough horses. Uncle Lem would need Bridger most of the time, taking the sick cowboy's place himself.

Uncle Lem saw how serious Pete looked. "I sure wish I had a horse for you, Pete," he said. "If you can hold out for ten days or two weeks, one of these hammerheads should be fit to ride."

Pete ran one big hand through his stubby, brown hair, then put his new Stetson back on. Well, he could always practice with his lariat—and he needed practice, too. But he wanted to get out and explore.

Close to the ranch house there was only flat alkali land covered with sagebrush. But off to the east the enormous range of the Sangre de Cristo mountains thrust up from the plain. Their dark, heavily wooded sides were cut with steep canyons and swift trout streams. And lying up against the range, just south of Crestone Needles, were the shimmering sand dunes—an expanse of real desert about which Uncle Lem had told him curious legends last winter. Uncle Lem had said that shepherds and whole flocks of sheep had been swallowed up by the sand. He had said that phantom web-footed horses were supposed to race across the ridges of the dunes by moonlight.

Pete's long legs could take him over to the dunes and back in a day, of course, but that wouldn't leave him much time for looking around. Besides, he liked company when he went exploring. Half the fun of going places, as far as he was concerned, was having somebody interesting to talk to.

"Uncle Lem," Pete said, "how about letting me go along with Juan while he's riding fence tomorrow? I can tell a broken barbed wire when I see one, just as well as you can."

Uncle Lem grinned. "Only trouble with that is that one rider goes one way and the other goes another when they're riding fence. You don't just locate a break where cows can get through. You have to fix it too. Do you know how to mend bobwire when it's broken?"

"I could learn," Pete said stubbornly.

"And besides that," Uncle Lem went on, "I've watched you with your lariat. Don't get sore when I say this, but do you think you could rope a steer and get him out if you found him bogged down in a swamp? There's nothing less grateful than one of those critters when he's rescued. I wouldn't want to find you waving around like a flag on some steer's horns. You gotta know cattle and bobwire and a few other things besides horses to do a cowhand's work."

Pete started to say again that he'd go along with Juan and learn, but he knew that was no good. His uncle did need two men who knew their business. He'd just have to make the best of it.

"Okay," Pete said with a smile. But he still hadn't given up the idea of doing something himself, instead of just sitting at a little private rodeo day after day while Slim topped off a horse for him to ride. He'd made up his mind he'd wangle himself a horse, and something to do on horseback, before the two weeks were up.

"Well, I might as well practice with my rope before supper," Pete said. He swung himself down to the ground with a rattle of his useless spurs. He'd been trying to learn the tricks of the lariat, but he still couldn't make the loop open the way he knew it should. He had a good right arm for pitching a screwball on a baseball diamond, and he had a keen eye. But time and again, his loop didn't open right when he made a cast at one of the two burros that wandered around his uncle's place.

As he turned toward the barn for his rope, he saw a peculiar-looking outfit rolling up the narrow road that led in from the highway five miles off. A team of horses was drawing what looked for all the world like an old-fashioned covered wagon.

In a minute, the wagon had pulled up in front of the kitchen door. The driver leaned out and shouted, "Hey, Lem! Hey, Clary!" Then he climbed down over the front wheel of the wagon and stretched himself. He was a small, dried-up-looking old man, and he made light, quick motions—like an aspen leaf in the breeze. "Hey, Clary!" he called again in a squeaky voice.

Pete walked toward the visitor and noticed that he wore moccasins instead of cowboy boots and that long, white hair curled out from his Mexican-type black sombrero.

"Hi," Pete said. "Aunt Clara's in the kitchen."

"What's she aunt of?" the old man said. "You? Never heard Lem Perkins was an uncle."

"Well, he is," Pete said, smiling.

Just then Aunt Clara called cheerily from the doorway, "If it isn't Hatsy! And just in time for supper, as usual. How long you staying this time?"

"Only overnight," the old man answered. "You know fishing's too good up around Crestone for me to waste time here."

"May I unhitch your horses?" Pete asked.

The old man looked Pete over shrewdly. "Clary, who's this yearling you've got here, all dressed up like a mail-order cowboy?"

"Why, that's our nephew from Chicago," Aunt Clara replied. "Hatsy, meet Pete Perkins. He's Lem's baby brother's son."

"Pleased to make your acquaintance," Hatsy said in a kind of grand manner that Pete liked. "Sure, you can unhitch the horses if you can tell one end from the other. They could stand some water, too, but don't let 'em drink their way clear down into the well."

After his first look at Hatsy, Pete had scarcely taken his eyes off the horses. They were unlike any animals he'd ever seen—small, beautifully shaped creatures, with liver-colored necks, shoulders, and forelegs. The hindquarters were almost white, with mahogany spots dotted here and there. The faces were white and the hind feet had white stockings. Under the dust from the road, Pete could see that their coats were well-groomed. Although they stood quietly resting, their heads and eyes were alert. These were finer horses than any he'd curried in the stable in Chicago—not the kind you'd expect to see pulling a covered wagon. And Pete was pretty sure he knew the breed. They were Apaloosas, a unique strain developed by the Nez Percé Indians up north and owned by only a few people.

With Hatsy's appraising eye on him, Pete un-hitched the horses, put on the halters that Hatsy got

"Hatsy, Meet Pete Perkins."

from the wagon, and led them to the watering trough into which water bubbled up under its own pressure, like a fountain, from the artesian well.

As the animals began to suck in the sweet, cool water that came from deep under the alkali flats, Pete turned to the old man and said, "Apaloosas, aren't they?"

"You know something about horses, don't you?" Hatsy said, and he didn't sound as tart as he had before.

"Are they broke to the saddle?" Pete asked hopefully.

"Wouldn't have a horse that wasn't broke to both saddle and harness," the old man replied. "Plenty of times I pack in to where the fishing is good after wagon country peters out."

Without asking, Pete knew that the horses had had enough water for the time being. Taking first one halter, then the other, he patted each horse as if he'd known it for a long time, then turned them toward the brand-new barn. "What do you call them?" he asked.

"Raindrop and Polkadot," Hatsy replied. "This here's Raindrop and that one's Polkadot."

"Do you mind if I give them a little oats after a while?"

"They do fine on nothing but grass," Hatsy said. "But Lem Perkins's oats never hurt 'em yet."

"I'll rub them down, too," Pete said.

He led the horses to the barn, which was still so new that it didn't have much of a horsy smell. At the door Old Chief, Uncle Lem's small, fat dog, greeted them and wagged his tail in delight. Chief was so old that he spent most of his time lying in the sun now, although he'd been a good pack-rat catcher in his day.

"Here's company for you, Chief," Pete said. And while Chief stood by for an hour, he curried and brushed the strange-looking coats of the two Apaloosas. He examined their hoofs for pebbles they might have picked up along the road. Unlike his uncle's horses, which needed only two shoes for their work on the range, these were shod in the more usual way on all four feet. Unwillingly, Pete stopped working over them when Aunt Clara rang the supper gong.

In spite of the arrival of the guest, supper was silent as usual. Pete was still surprised at how little ranch people talked during meals. But they were hungry, and food was to eat. Afterward, if there was time, talking would start. Tonight Pete was even more surprised by his Aunt Clara. She let Hatsy eat the entire meal with his black sombrero on, although she'd told Pete the first day that she had a rule nobody could wear his Stetson in *her* house—not even Uncle Lem.

Aunt Clara saw Pete staring and said to him quietly, "Hatsy never takes his hat off!"

Presently Uncle Lem said, "What you going to do this summer, Hatsy? Go prospecting for uranium or something? I hear that's the latest fad."

"Thanks for the idea. Maybe I'll try it," Hatsy answered. "But in between times I'm mainly going to try some new bait I got last winter from an Indian in the Arizona desert."

"Fish taken to growing on cactuses down there lately?" Uncle Lem asked with a straight face.

"Just like uranium's taken to sprouting out of the hills up here," Hatsy replied. Aunt Clara snorted. Then she got up to clear the table, and the hands filed out to the bunkhouse.

"Now would be the time to set out on that screen porch I haven't got," said Aunt Clara. "We were fixing to put it on when the barn burned down, Hatsy. Not that you seem to mind the mosquitoes. Or maybe that's why you're so skinny. You been donating blood to pests for the last seventy-five years, sleeping out the way you do."

Hatsy cackled, "At least I don't get rheumaticks the way some folks do." And then he added seriously, "I sure am sorry for all your bad luck."

"It's hard on Pete here, too," Uncle Lem said. "He likes horses and he came out expecting to ride right along with me and the hands. But I haven't an extra animal on the place that's gentle enough so I'd risk anybody but Slim on it. He's the only cowpoke alive that's made of nothing but rawhide and rubber. It looks like it'll be a couple of weeks before Slim gets one of those hammerheads so he can understand Chicago lingo."

Pete didn't really mind when they teased him about being a tenderfoot and about the pancake saddles he'd been used to back home. He could ride Western style, too.

Hatsy was silent for a minute. Then he said, "Seeing your chuck is so good, Clary, I might arrange to stay over for an extra day and let Pete see how he likes the fit of my saddle on Raindrop."

"Hey, that's swell!" Pete said. "Thanks a lot. The saddle ought to fit, too. We're just about the same size."

"It's up to you, Hatsy," Uncle Lem said. "It would sure be nice for Pete. You know you're always welcome here."

"Especially since you always leave the sheets as clean as you find 'em," Aunt Clara added.

"Speaking of that," Hatsy said, "I guess Pete has bedded down the Apaloosies, so I'll just crawl into my soogans before the best sleeping part of the night gets too far past."

Pete went out and helped the old man get the quilts he called soogans from the covered wagon and watched while he laid them out on a tarpaulin on the ground under the wagon.

"I'll be out early in the morning," Pete said.

"Don't be too sure you'll find me right here," Hatsy said. "Nobody's beat me out of bed since Pecos Bill tipped the Rio Grande on end to wet his whistle."

Pete returned to the house hoping to get his aunt and uncle to answer the questions he wanted to ask about Hatsy. Who was he? Why did he roam around in his wagon? How did they know him so well? And why did he do so many curious things—like wearing moccasins, and a hat at the table? But the others had gone to bed already. So Pete turned in, too, full of thoughts about the Apaloosas and the day in the saddle he had been promised.

CHAPTER TWO

The next morning when Pete awoke, he knew it was later than the other days he'd been on the ranch, and still there were no sounds of stirring in the house. Puzzled, he dressed and went out through the kitchen where the breakfast fire had not been started in the range. The clock on the shelf told him it was six, and he knew his aunt and uncle were supposed to be up at four-thirty.

Outside, he was even more surprised to find Hatsy still under the wagon, but squatting on his bedroll, bareheaded and with his hat in his hands. Now Pete saw that Hatsy was bald. The long white hair that showed beneath his hat came only from around the side and back of his head.

"I thought you never took your hat off," Pete said.

"Ordinarily, I'd say that what I did was nobody's business but mine," Hatsy retorted. "But you're kind of a tenderfoot, so I guess I can allow a little for you butting in where you weren't asked."

The old man paused and lifted up his stiff, shiny sombrero for inspection. "How do you like the new hatband?" he said. "A rattler crawled into bed with me last night to keep warm. In case you don't know,

25

rattlers in your bed won't strike you if you take it easy getting out. Well, I took it easy, but I just thought I'd make him pay for his lodging by lending me his skin for a while."

There, in place of the beadwork hatband he had worn the day before, was a rattlesnake skin. "Did you sew it on?" Pete asked.

"Course not," Hatsy replied scornfully. "Anybody knows that there's a kind of glue inside a rattlesnake skin. It just naturally holds tight when it dries."

As Hatsy started to put on his newly decorated sombrero, Pete saw a big scar in the center of his bald pate.

"How did you get that scar?" he asked before he thought.

"Never saw a young feller so curious about other people's business," Hatsy snorted. "But I guess there's no harm in telling. When I was just a shaver, younger than you are and just as green, I got mixed up with a band of Ute Indians. They were hungry, and had come over to South Fork for some horses to eat. They weren't particular about whether the horses were running wild or had brands on them. They just liked horse meat. And from the looks of them, a few good steaks wouldn't have done them any harm.

"My old man had dabbed his brand on quite a few mustangs along the Rio Grande, and he felt real

"How Do You Like the New Hatband?"

property proud. So he got into an argument with the
Utes when he saw his brand on a pony they were
fixing to carve up for supper. That was the end of
my dad, and almost the end of me. One of the Utes
had a gun, but he wasn't much of a shot. He just
creased my skull." Hatsy pointed to the scar. "And
then he raised my hair as a souvenir. Reckon he was
so mad when his supper was interrupted that he got
careless and didn't make sure I was dead. He just
hung my scalp on his belt and lit out."

Pete felt his own crew haircut bristling as he listened. He'd never really thought before how it
would feel to be scalped, and he didn't like it.

"I came around all right after the Utes were gone,"
Hatsy went on. "I never got my hair back, but I got
used to that. What did bother me was the creasing
job on my skull. Anything touching that place sends
me plumb loco. You can knock me out, it seems, if
you hit me there with a feather. So I got me a hat
that doesn't dent so easy. And I wear it."

"Anybody ever catch the Utes?" Pete asked.

"No, they made themselves mighty scarce for quite
a while. I've been all over Ute country, just kind of
looking casually for that hair of mine. But I never
seen it and never will. Got to know those Indians
pretty well, though, while I was looking. And they
can have my scalp. It's about all they have left in this
world. The fact is, my own ranch had been part of

the Ute hunting grounds before some white men took it away from them and sold it to me."

"You used to own a ranch?" Pete asked.

"Why not?" the old man replied. "But I sold it a few years back, and now I just go 'round, seeing the country and staying where it's cool in summer and warm in winter."

Hatsy got up to heave his bedroll into the wagon, and Pete gave him a hand. Then suddenly Pete remembered how late it was.

"Hey, what do you suppose happened to everybody?" Pete said. "They're late getting up this morning. I'm starved, too."

"I tell Lem he's got the wrong name for this ranch," Hatsy answered. "Instead of calling it the Lazy B-5, he ought to call it the 5-B-Lazy. He never gets up till six o'clock on Sundays. Let's go in there and raise the dickens about breakfast."

Just then Pete heard Aunt Clara rattling in the kitchen. "I'd better go look after Raindrop and Polkadot," he said.

Hatsy came along to the barn. As they fed and watered the horses, Old Chief tagged along, full of delight at the attention both Pete and Hatsy paid him.

Finally Pete got a chance to ask, "What kind of flies do you use for trout in this country?"

"That'd be telling," the old man replied. "I never

told anybody what bait I used for fish, any more than I'd have told them years back what bait I used for beaver."

"Beaver?" Pete was puzzled.

"Sure," Hatsy went on. "There used to be plenty of beaver in the mountains, and anybody knows you have to trap them with castor bait. The castor is a gland a beaver grows under his skin. So you use one part of one beaver to trap another. It's the fixing of the castor that's the secret."

Pete was more and more interested in this old man who seemed to be an endless mine of new information. He wanted to ask a lot of questions about beaver, but he was beginning to work out a whole plan in his mind.

"Do you always go fishing alone?" Pete said.

"Well, years back I had a partner, but ever since he got into an argument with the wrong end of a mule, he's been pushing up daisies. You got any ideas?"

"Well, I thought maybe you might be able to use some help around your camp, and Uncle Lem doesn't have much of anything for me to do here. I could come back to the ranch when Slim has a horse broke so I can help ride fence," Pete said.

"Ever been camping?" the old man asked.

"I don't know whether *you'd* call it camping, but I do," Pete answered. "The Boys' Club I belong to has a place where it takes kids in the summer and in the winter, too. We used to sleep out in the summertime, and we learned how to cook our own food. In the winter we stayed in a cabin and skied all the time."

"Sounds kind of like a dude ranch to me," Hatsy said in a joking sort of way.

"I suppose it does," Pete replied. "But it wasn't a fancy place. We had to do all our own work. If you take me along, I'll show you I know how to do a lot of things."

"I'll think it over," Hatsy said. "I take my time making my mind up, but once it's made it stays made."

"I guess I'd better water your horses now," Pete said, feeling some hope that Hatsy would take him on the trip. "Then I'll turn Polkadot into the pasture for today, and I'll tie Raindrop to the wagon, so he'll be ready to saddle after breakfast. Or maybe you were planning to ride with us?" Pete wished the old man would come along.

But Hatsy said, "No, I figure I'll mend up some harness and check over my fishing tackle, ready to move on tomorrow."

When Pete brought Raindrop back to be tied, the old man had his saddle on the tailgate of the wagon. Beside it lay a Navaho Indian blanket with angular designs in red and black and gray. Pete reached out and felt the soft texture. The Indian blankets he'd seen had all been stiff and heavy, but this was something different, and it looked far too valuable to be used as he suspected Hatsy used it.

"What's this for?" he asked.

"A saddle blanket, of course," Hatsy replied. "I got it off a Navaho friend of mine. His wife made it, and she did it the right way. It's not tourist stuff."

Pete spread the blanket out and examined it carefully.

"See the place that looks like she made a mistake?" Hatsy said. "All Navaho blankets have a mistake on purpose. The Indians do it that way for good luck. If you keep one of these things washed, it's the best saddle blanket a horse can have, and it wears longer, too."

A minute later Aunt Clara stepped out and whacked the iron triangle which hung near the door. The iron rang like a bell, calling the men in to breakfast. Before they had quite finished their hotcakes with fried eggs on top and ham on the side, they heard the sound of an auto engine in the road.

"Wonder who's out visiting this time of a Sunday?" Aunt Clara said as she got up to look through the window. "Lem, it's strangers. Coming in a jeep."

When the jeep pulled up at the house, a heavy-set man in mountain boots and city hat climbed out of the seat next to the driver. He called:

"Where's Lem Perkins?"

"I guess I'm the one you're looking for," Uncle Lem answered slowly. "What can I do for you?"

"I want to buy a couple of horses," the stranger said, "and I heard you were selling. I'm going to camp out in the Sangre de Cristos all summer—doctor's orders." And then he added, "Moore's my name."

"Glad to make your acquaintance," Uncle Lem said. "I sold all the horses I could afford to sell, but maybe if your price is right I could spare a couple of ponies from the rough string. They'll be okay for mountain work in a week or two."

"That's no good," said Moore, plainly showing annoyance. "I'm not going to spend my summer bronco-busting. I came here to buy a good riding horse and a pack horse, and I intend to buy them. Now name your price."

Pete looked from the stranger to his uncle, and he guessed that Uncle Lem was thinking about the payments on the barn. He couldn't blame Uncle Lem for trying to get out of the debt he'd been put into by the fire. But Pete could see plainly what was going to happen. Uncle Lem would sell Bridger, his own horse. Then he would put Slim out on the range, because Uncle Lem was too old to ride the rough horses himself. That would mean Slim wouldn't have much time to break a horse for Pete to ride. It

would be maybe a month or so before Pete got a
horse. "If ever," he said to himself dismally.

Just then Hatsy pulled Pete's shirt and said,
"Come here, son. I made up my mind about
sumpin."

When the two of them reached the watering
trough, Hatsy said, "You go pack your stuff. Looks
like hoss-flesh is disappearing fast around this place
—almost the way it did around my father's place
when the Utes got hungry. I know how it feels to
lose something. Didn't I lose my scalp besides my
dad? You're set afoot for the best part of the summer,
son. But I've got an idea where you can get a good
pony. If you'll come along, like you said, and help
around my camp for a few weeks, I'll guarantee
you'll come back riding a horse of your own."

"I don't get it, Hatsy," Pete said. "I'd like to go
fishing with you. But where does the horse come in?
I'm not going to take one of yours."

"You sure ain't," said Hatsy. "I broke them, the
way you're going to break yours, and they're mine.
But don't worry, you'll get one."

Pete had read about horse stealing, and for a moment he looked at Hatsy doubtfully. "I still don't
get it," he said.

"You wait and see," Hatsy replied. "It will all be
fair and square. And I'm not going to give you anything—except that both of us will have a good time.

Now you go pack. I'll corral Lem and Clara. All you'll have to do is ride back here every few days to get the mail from your folks and pick up supplies we may be running out of. My wagon has a lot of stuff in it but it's not a chain store and I didn't know I was going to have company."

Pete felt his spirits suddenly rising.

"Hey, Clary!" Hatsy called. "Come here."

Aunt Clara moved away from the jeep, where the stranger named Moore was still talking to Uncle Lem. Hatsy told her he wanted to take Pete with him for a fishing trip. "I'll see he doesn't fall in the crick," he finished.

"Trust Hatsy," Aunt Clara said to Pete. "He's always scheming up something. The funny thing is, some of his schemes work out. So far as I'm concerned, you can go, Pete—provided you bring me back a mess of trout. Better ask Lem, though. When are you leaving?"

"I figure we can be ready right after we get our noon bait under our belts," Hatsy said.

"Noon bait?" Pete said, puzzled.

"Dinner—to boys from Chicago," Hatsy snapped.

"I thought you were going to ride Raindrop, Pete," Aunt Clara said.

"I can wait to ride him till we get our camp set up," Pete replied.

Hatsy looked at Pete and winked. "Don't worry,

Clary," he said. "Pete'll get plenty of riding. I'll go talk to Lem."

As Hatsy and Pete approached the jeep, Moore's angry voice rose. "All right, I'll take the burro, then. I haven't got time to chase all over this valley looking for a pack horse."

"What's your hurry, mister?" Uncle Lem said quietly. "I thought you were supposed to be taking it easy for your health."

"I guess you're right," Moore said. "Doctor told me I was too nervous." He began to count out bills and handed them to Uncle Lem.

Uncle Lem asked Slim to get Bridger from the pasture, then he said to Pete, "Mr. Moore's bought the gray burro, too. Do you want to get her and bring her over? He's going to pack up right now."

As Uncle Lem went to the house to write out the bill of sale for Moore, Hatsy fell in step with him. And when Pete came back, leading the burro, Hatsy called, "We're all set. Clary will lend you some soogans."

Moore and his driver, whom he had not bothered to introduce, were pulling some boxes and bundles out of the jeep. In a short while they had a pack saddle on the burro and the load almost ready. It seemed to Pete a surprisingly small pack for a man who was going to camp out all summer.

"Aren't you traveling pretty light?" he asked.

Moore Paid Uncle Lem for the Horse

Moore simply gave him an irritated look, and while his companion finished throwing a diamond hitch on the pack, Moore flung a saddle on Bridger. Then he said something to the jeep driver Pete couldn't hear, swung into the saddle and was off, without even a friendly farewell. Uncle Lem gave the burro a swat on her hindquarters, and she tagged along obediently behind Bridger across the alkali plain toward the mountains.

"Queer characters," Uncle Lem said as the jeep went off down the road. "I hope that fellow Moore takes better care of the animals than I'm afraid he will."

Uncle Lem went off toward the barn.

"I wonder where Moore's going to camp," Pete said.

"I wonder a lot of things," Hatsy said. "Fer instance, what a couple of tough-looking hombres like that are doing with a fancy bow and arrow set in their jeep. Just happened to notice it when they were packing up."

"Well, anyway," Pete said, "what do we do next?"

"Next thing is to pack up ourselves," Hatsy answered. "Go and get your stuff ready."

Pete sprinted to the house. Half an hour later Hatsy came to the door of Pete's room and surveyed the chaos. Everything out of two suitcases was strung over the floor and bed.

"Looks to me like you've got enough equipment there to outfit an expedition to the middle of the Sahara Desert," Hatsy said. "All you've forgotten is Clary's old organ."

Pete felt embarrassed and didn't know what to say.

"All you need is a pair of blankets and a tarp," Hatsy explained. "Clary said she'd rustle them up for you. Then put in an extra shirt and pants, a jacket, slicker, a couple of changes of socks, and something besides those high-heeled boots to hike in."

"I've only got my city shoes," Pete said in alarm.

"All right, don't worry. I'll fix you up. Your foot looks about the same size as mine," Hatsy replied, and added, "Ask Clary for an old flour sack. That'll be your war-bag. Put your toothbrush and any little gadgets you want in that, same as any cowhand does on the roundup. Come on, we'll get the flour sack and something else we'll need, too."

After Aunt Clara had given Pete his war-bag, Hatsy asked her for some string. She handed him a small ball of twine, but Hatsy wasn't satisfied.

"Don't be so stingy," he complained. "I want lots of string, and you've got it. Everybody this side of Wagon Wheel Gap knows you're the string-savingest woman in the valley. There isn't a piece of twine that's come onto this ranch in twenty years that isn't on one of those big balls you keep in your hall closet. I want as much as you'll let me have, and I don't promise to bring it back, either. I want all the bright colored rags you'll let me have, too."

"Hatsy, you've been out in the sun too long. I knew no good would come of your taking your hat off this morning." Aunt Clara stood there with her hands on her hips and looked at the old man in amazement. Pete was equally astonished.

"Come on, don't string me along. Just give me the string," Hatsy said.

"You sure are up to something," Aunt Clara said, shaking her head in perplexity. "Well, all right, the string might as well be used for something. But if you think I'm going to beg you to tell me what crazy scheme you've got, you're wrong."

She opened the hall closet where there were several shelves holding balls of different kinds of string and twine, some of them as big as basketballs. Hatsy helped himself to three that seemed to be made up of the strongest twine. When he asked her again for the rags, Aunt Clara complained:

"Hatsy, I do declare, you've gone plumb loco!" She couldn't hide her curiosity any longer. "What in the world do you want rags for?"

"Well, you see it's this way. I'm not as young as I used to be. In the morning the ground's kind of chilly on my feet when I pull them out of my soogans. And I thought a nice rag rug would come in handy. Figured I'd make myself one, with me doing the planning and Pete doing the weaving."

For a minute Pete didn't know whether to believe Hatsy or not. But, by the way Aunt Clara said, "Oh, pshaw!" he knew Hatsy was kidding again. Sooner or later, Pete knew he'd find out what the string and rags were for.

CHAPTER THREE

HATSY'S SCHEME

What with one thing and another, Pete and Hatsy didn't leave the ranch till midafternoon. But at last the old man called "Giddap!" to the Apaloosas, and Pete felt a sense of real excitement as they headed off across country toward the sand dunes.

There, ahead, lay the great eastern wall of the San Luis Valley, the Sangre de Cristo mountain range, that rose up at points more than fourteen thousand feet above sea level. Crestone Needles to the left and Mount Blanca to the right were still topped with snow. Below them, at the edge of the valley lay the eight square miles of creamy-white sand dunes that Pete was so eager to explore.

As the sun began to drop behind the mountains to the west, a great change came over the Sangre de Cristos and the sand dunes. The tops of the peaks, and the dunes, too, turned bright red in the sunset.

"Look!" Pete said in amazement. "A minute ago they were white. What color are they anyway?"

"You can't rightly say what color something is that changes all the time," Hatsy answered. "Sometimes they look brown. Later in the evening they'll look purple. The dunes change shape, too. They're never the same any two days running."

"I bet they're worth exploring," Pete said.

"A person's life is worth more," Hatsy said quite seriously. "People have gone into those dunes and never come back. You can poke around the edges all right, but you never want to go in very far. We'll be camping close to them for a good while now, so you'll have plenty of chance to explore the edges."

"Is that where we're going to get me a horse?" Pete asked. "Why, it's almost on our ranch."

"I guess Lem told you the legends that maybe came down from the Indians," Hatsy said. "They say that every bright moonlight night and sometimes just before sundown, you can see giant web-footed horses running on the ridges of the dunes. Of course, maybe the wind blowing the sand only made it look like the tails and manes of horses running, but the fact is, there *are* wild horses around the edges of the dunes. Only they are small, instead of being giants. And you might say they were kind of web-footed. They've got extra-big hoofs. And when it comes to running in sand, they can beat any horses alive."

"You mean you've really seen them?" Pete exclaimed.

"Sure, I've watched 'em many a time, but I never could catch up with them. They always head out into the dunes when you chase 'em. An ordinary horse sinks down in the sand. Cowboys say the sand dune mustangs are too small to bother trying to break for ranch work, and they think their big feet look funny. A real cowpoke wouldn't be seen dead on a horse like that. But I've got a hunch that one of these ponies is worth a corral full of most others when it comes to work in mountain country. They're plenty big enough for cutting horses, too, and maybe even for calf-roping."

"But can you just go out and take one of them without asking anybody?"

"Sure," Hatsy answered. "Nobody owns them. The government doesn't care about them, and so far as ranchers are concerned, they're only a nuisance. If you can catch one, he's yours for the taking."

Pete felt a little disappointed. If a cowboy wouldn't be seen on one of the horses, he wasn't sure he wanted to be seen on one either. He lapsed into silence as he sat beside Hatsy on the hard board wagon seat. Hatsy urged his horses on faster now, and he turned them soon onto rising land at the north end of the dunes. The going was more difficult here, the ground rougher. Hatsy had to drive with care as he edged the wagon around crumbling boulders and clumps of aspen that dotted the lowest slopes of Crestone Needles.

Then, he turned sharply to the right and downhill. Suddenly, they were between the sand dunes and the grassy mouth of a canyon along the sides of which light was retreating toward the tops of the peaks. Before long the brief mountain twilight would be falling.

"Hatsy!" Pete almost shouted as he pointed down toward the canyon. "Horses!"

"Well, I'll be!" Hatsy exclaimed with genuine surprise. He slowed the wagon to a stop. "I never thought we'd see them mustangs so soon."

"They don't look wild," Pete said. "They're not running away."

"They don't know we're here," Hatsy replied. "They haven't caught sight of us yet and they couldn't hear the wagon coming. Listen to the way the dunes are moaning and groaning under the wind. That noise sounds real big down where they are. Besides, the wind's blowing toward us, so they can't smell us. Just the same, you'd better look 'em over and see if there's a pony among 'em that you like. They'll see us any minute now."

The band, probably about thirty in all, were mustangs—buckskin colored, with darker manes and tails and a dark stripe along the spine. A stallion, who was their leader, kept a watchful eye on the mares and their colts. One younger stallion grazed a little to one side by himself.

Hatsy pointed to the young stallion and said, "In another year that fellow will be full grown. If we can catch *him,* you're all set."

The misgivings Pete had felt earlier disappeared. Certainly no cowboy would be ashamed to ride that horse. He was well-shaped and he moved with such ease that Pete didn't even think to look to see if he had big feet.

"I thought you said they were small horses," Pete said. "They look plenty large enough to me."

"They are plenty large enough," Hatsy answered. "But they stand less than fourteen hands high, and not one of 'em weighs seven hundred pounds, except maybe the old stallion. They're a little smaller than my Apaloosies, but there's no use to a big horse unless you need a big horse. A good horse is a lot better," he concluded as he gave a perky nod toward his team.

Pete hadn't taken his eyes off the young stallion. "Do you honestly think we can catch him?" he said.

"I couldn't ask for better."

"We'll know when we've caught him," Hatsy answered. "Now we gotta pitch camp in a hurry." He clucked at the team to start them down the short slope that separated them from the wild mustangs.

Instantly the old stallion below trumpeted an alarm, and in a few seconds the whole herd had fled up into the dunes and disappeared behind the first high ridge.

Pete stood up in the seat for one last look at the young stallion. He was determined to see the horse

again. He wanted it more than he'd ever wanted
anything before.

"Get your mind on setting up camp," Hatsy said.
"We better move fast."

Pete had already learned that night came suddenly
in the mountain country. He jumped out of the
wagon as it pulled to a stop, and began collecting
firewood.

While Hatsy unhitched and tethered the horses,
Pete got a fire going. By the time it was dark, Hatsy
had prepared a hot meal of canned beans, canned
tomatoes, bacon, and coffee, and Pete had cut the
apple pie that Aunt Clara had put under the wagon
seat just before they left.

All this time, the two of them had talked very
little. Pete was pleased that he'd been able to do
things with few instructions from Hatsy. Now, with
supper over and the bedrolls made up under the
wagon, Hatsy squatted down cross-legged by the fire
and Pete stretched out on his stomach, just enjoying
life.

"Want to know why I tied the horses instead of
putting the hobbles on?" Hatsy asked. "This is why.
I don't know if you noticed as we came down the
slope, but the creek that runs out of the canyon dis-
appears just below here."

Pete had been too much interested in the wild
mustangs to notice anything. He shook his head.

"It's called Lost Creek," Hatsy went on. "It just sinks into the sand at the edge of the dunes. And right there is a mess of quicksand. One time there was a party camped here that didn't know about it. They hobbled their horses, and when the fellows woke up in the morning, the animals *and* the wagon had plumb sunk out of sight. So I tether my Apaloosies high and dry. You watch out, too. The mustangs are wise to the quicksand, of course. They always come to water where the ground is solid."

Sleeping under the wagon cut off a lot of the stars overhead, but Pete guessed he couldn't have been happier, even if he could have seen them. As he took his cowboy boots off to put under his head for a pillow, Hatsy tossed him something.

"These moccasins will be a lot easier on your feet than your boots while you're walking," he said. "You'll be afoot a good bit till your pony's ready to ride."

Pete examined the moccasins. They had heavy rawhide soles, the way desert Indians made them, but the uppers were soft.

"You can wade in these, too," Hatsy said. "And it's a lot easier than having your boots full of water. Good for fishing."

"How are we going to catch that horse, Hatsy?" Pete asked. "I'm not very good at roping yet."

"Not going to use a rope," Hatsy answered. "We'll

use string instead. Now go to sleep."

Pete tried to obey the instructions, but it was a long time before he quit wondering what Hatsy's plan was. How could anyone catch a horse with string?

CHAPTER FOUR

HORSE TRAP

After making a mess of flapjacks for breakfast, Hatsy explained the plan he had worked out. They would go upstream looking for a place to build a trap—a horse trap to catch Pete's mustang.

First they would need a box canyon, and Hatsy remembered there *was* one somewhere up Lost Creek. It was not a big box canyon—just a small flat place with rocks rising up on three sides too steeply for a horse to climb. A barred gate on the fourth side would make it into an enclosure as good as a corral. The main job was going to be to get the horse into this corral, after they had made the gate. And Hatsy said he had a plan for that, too.

With Pete riding Raindrop and Hatsy on Polkadot, they picked their way up the canyon above camp. The going was slow, and they kept well away from the bank of the creek wherever they could, pushing through the alders and pines and chokecherry bushes. It wasn't more than half an hour, though, before they came to a place where the slope down to the creek was gentle. There in the muddy bank they saw large hoofprints of the sand dune mustangs. Those hoofprints were as big as Hatsy's flapjacks, Pete thought.

"Good," Hatsy said. "This country is looking familiar to me now. I'm sure you'll find the box canyon up ahead not too far. You go on by yourself and locate it. I got things to do at camp. After you make sure the canyon is there, come on back. You can't get lost if you just follow the creek downhill and keep the dunes on your left. Meet you at camp when the sun's straight up."

Pete was excited. He was on his own in strange mountain country. And he was getting ready to catch a horse of his own. He rode on slowly, up along the noisy, rushing creek. Still there were no big outcroppings of rock, no side canyons that answered Hatsy's description. He glanced at the sun. It was high now, and Hatsy would have chuck ready. Pete was hungry, but he was determined not to turn back until he had found what he was looking for.

At last, he rode up out of the canyon bottom on the north side where the going seemed a bit clearer. As he topped a slight ridge, he saw ahead, on the other side of the creek, a large rock formation. He studied it intently as he rode closer. Then, when he came directly opposite it, he was sure it was the box canyon Hatsy had sent him to find.

Turning Raindrop, he worked downhill to the creek, splashed across and up onto the other bank. The place fitted Hatsy's description exactly. Pete rode once around inside the secluded spot and saw that bars could easily be placed across the narrow opening, making it into a corral. But he still couldn't figure out how horses could be guided into it—especially wild horses that would be almost certain not even to notice it if they were in flight.

Now Pete doubled back toward camp, keeping high up on the south side of the creek. From time to time, he stopped and looked at the shimmering mountain of sand which he could see ahead of him and off to his left. A wind played along the ridges, raising little plumes of sand and then letting them drop. As far as he could see there was sand on that side. On his right was the mountain, rising endlessly. This was the loneliest place he'd ever been in.

He was glad enough to get back to camp at last where Hatsy had been keeping his chuck ready for him in the Dutch oven at the side of the fire.

As he rode into the clearing, he couldn't quite believe what he saw. There sat Hatsy, cross-legged on the ground, tearing an old red-and-white tablecloth into strips and stuffing the pieces into a bulging gunnysack.

"What in the world are you doing?" Pete exclaimed.

"Making a pillow for that horse we're going to catch. You want him to be nice and comfy, don't you?" the old man said with a chortle. "Where you been all this time?"

"Prospecting for uranium," Pete said in the same tone.

Hatsy laughed. "Okay, we're even. Did you find the box canyon?"

"Yep," Pete said. "It's a little farther away than you thought, but it's there all right. And it's a beaut."

As Pete ate his corned beef hash, Hatsy kept right on tearing up rags. Pete decided he could keep from asking questions just as long as Hatsy could keep from answering. For a long time neither of them said a word. Pete could hardly keep from laughing. At last he got up, went and sat down next to Hatsy, and without a word started tearing up an old apron from the pile of rags Aunt Clara had given them. Hatsy gave him an appraising look and kept right on ripping up the odd pieces of cloth.

In an hour the rags were all torn into strips. Pete, with a straight face, got up and reached into the wagon. He pulled out Hatsy's spare shirt and sat down again. As Hatsy looked up, Pete pretended he was going to tear the shirt.

"Hey! you Chicago gangster! Taking the shirt off my back! I give up."

Now Hatsy explained what the rags were for, and the huge balls of string which Aunt Clara had given them, too. These were the makings of the horse trap.

The string, attached to trees and shrubs, would be

stretched out from either side of the box canyon in the shape of an enormous funnel. The rags would be hung from the string at intervals. Hatsy swore that the rags waving in the wind would make just as good a fence as barbed wire or the heavy posts around a horse-breaking corral. The horses, seeing the bright, moving rags, would be too frightened to approach, let alone break through the one strand of string.

"But before we build the string fence," Hatsy said, "we've got to put a gate in the box canyon. You get the point, don't you? We'll drive a bunch of the horses into the mouth of the string funnel. We'll stay behind them and keep hazing them toward the box canyon where the little end of the funnel is. When they get into the box, we just shut the gate quick, and there we are."

"You honestly mean that the two of us and a string fence can trap a bunch of horses as easy as that?" Pete asked in amazement.

"I sure do," Hatsy replied. "It's an old trick that's been used in rough country ever since horses was invented. What's more, you're going to do all the hazing yourself. As a general thing it takes a bigger crew to round up mustangs this way, and they make fancier gates than we're going to have. I'll have to stay right there at the box canyon all the time, so as to be on the spot to close the gate when you get the horses into the box. It will be your job to keep them traveling up the funnel. It will be kind of hard, but I think you can work it."

Pete still couldn't quite believe that such a simple stunt would work. But he was willing to try anything. All the next day, while they were building the gate, he got more and more excited about the idea. He was pleased, too, when Hatsy commented that he handled an ax pretty well for a city slicker.

With Pete chopping down sturdy evergreen trees for the gate, and Hatsy lashing them in place with rawhide thongs, they soon had a rough set of bars constructed. When the long poles were pulled back, the gate would be open. But a few quick movements could push the poles across the opening, into rests, and the poles would make a solid fence, through which no horse could break. A thick bush stood at one side of the gate. Behind it Hatsy could hide while the horses were approaching, so as not to frighten them back. Once they were inside, he could push the bars into place, closing the final trap on them.

"Here's your corral," Hatsy announced, when the gate was finished. "Now you want to clear away the brush around the edges inside. You want a clear space to work in while you're gentling your horse. But don't cut down that piñon tree there in the middle. Just trim the branches off and leave about four feet of the trunk standing. That's going to be your

Hatsy Lashed the Poles in Place

snubbing post."

Pete knew what the snubbing post was for. He'd seen Slim use one at the ranch when he was roping a bronc. Slim would turn the rope around the post once, and the friction of the rope on the post helped him hold even the most cantankerous horse.

Working fast, Pete cleared the brush and piñon limbs. Then he flopped down flat on his back on the grass inside the corral. He was tired. His hands were sore, because he wasn't used to swinging an ax. But he had never been more pleased with anything in his life. Only one thing concerned him a little. Was he sneaking back here into the mountains to do some bronc busting which he knew very well his Uncle Lem didn't want him to do?

At last he confessed to Hatsy what was on his mind.

"You don't need to worry, son," the old man said. "You're not going to fork any bronc that's in a buckin' frame of mind. You're going to gentle your horse different from the way Slim and most other peelers work. And you'll have a better horse and more skin left on you when you're done. You just wait and see. You're not going to do anything that would curl your uncle's hair."

Just then they heard a crashing in the brush farther up the creek. In a moment, a horse came into view. It was Bridger with Moore in the saddle.

Before Pete or Hatsy could say "Howdy," Moore

shouted angrily at them, "So it's you. I wondered who had been making all the racket down here. You know I came out here to rest. What are you doing here anyway?"

"That question can go two ways," Hatsy replied. "But I'll tell you how it is. Me and Pete are fixing to start a rackabore ranch."

"A *what?*"

"If you haven't seen any rackabores yet, it's because you haven't gone high enough up on Crestone Needles."

Moore looked baffled, and Pete felt that way, too. Neither one said anything for a while.

"Well, all I've got to say is, I want to be let alone. Catch your whatever-it-is someplace else. I've got to have peace and quiet." Moore turned Bridger and rode back in the direction from which he had come.

"Friendly cuss, isn't he?" Hatsy said. "Hope he meets a rackabore some day."

"What in blue blazes is a rackabore?" Pete asked.

Hatsy, keeping a perfectly straight face, told him that it was a mountain varmint with short legs on the left side—shorter than the legs on the right. This made it easy for it to walk along the side of a mountain. Eating as they went, rackabores moved round and round a peak, always going in the same direction and always climbing higher. When they got to the top of the peak they couldn't go any farther. So all you had to do to catch them was chase them to the top.

"Only one thing worries me," Pete said. "We have the wrong kind of corral for rackabores. The ground is level. Will we have to make stilts for their left legs?"

"Yeah, or we can dig holes for them to rest their right feet in," Hatsy said. "You know what a rackabore says about this time every day? It just bawls out, 'Chuck-chuck-chuck.' Let's go. We gotta get our beauty rest so we can put up that string fence tomorrow."

Pete grinned, and went to saddle the horses.

CHAPTER FIVE

A BREAK IN THE FENCE

Working together on foot next day, Pete and Hatsy strung out several thousand yards of string in both directions from the mouth of the box canyon. One line of the string went north across the creek, up along the side of Crestone Needles, ending near an abandoned mine. The other wing of the trap went off to the southwest along the mountainside, nearly as far as a small creek, which Hatsy said flowed into Lost Creek. On the other side of this creek rose the dunes.

Pete lugged the gunnysack of torn rags over his shoulder and Hatsy carried a big ball of string in his arms. Every few feet, between the trees and shrubs around which Hatsy looped the string, Pete tied rags to the line. It was slow work in the hot sun, but by evening they were through.

Back at camp, Hatsy said, "Starting tomorrow, we'll try to locate the mustangs. When we find them —maybe it won't be for a few days—you'll stalk them, slow but steady, shoving them toward the trap. As soon as we've found them, I'll circle around to the box canyon and be waiting there to close the gate. Your job will be to keep them headed the right way

and to split the herd up if you can. There ain't room
for even half the herd in that corral of ours, and even
then they'll be packed as tight as beans in a can."

The full force of the idea that he had to haze the
wild horses all by himself suddenly struck Pete. He
had never rounded up cattle, let alone mustangs,
and he knew horses were a lot smarter. He wondered
if he could do the job.

"Do you think I can do it?" Pete asked.

"You want a pony, don't you?" Hatsy grumbled.
"So you have to get him. I can't be in two places at
once, and somebody's gotta close that gate. In case
you hadn't noticed, I'm no yearling. My days of chasing mustangs was over quite a while back—I'd say
even a good bit before you started adding to the general confusion in Chicago."

"Okay, lay off, Hatsy," Pete said. "I'll bet I get
that corral full of horses before you even remember
where it is."

"Don't be in too much of a hurry," Hatsy said, "or
you'll stampede them clear across Mosca Pass to the
other side of the mountains. I mean that. You gotta
be careful and patient."

But as Hatsy gave his warning, there was friendliness in his snappy little eyes.

Next morning before it was light Pete and Hatsy
rode the Apaloosas up the wooded side of the mountain immediately above the dunes. As they rose high-

er and higher it seemed to Pete that more and more
of the world opened out below him. He had the crazy
notion that if he could only get up high enough he
could see everything.

There below was the flat valley stretching dozens
and dozens of miles to the north and west and south.
There was his uncle's spread with the ranch buildings. Hundreds of cattle dotted the range land.

"Now we're above the dunes. Maybe we can see
something," Hatsy said as he lifted the handkerchief
which hung around his neck and wiped his sweaty
face. The ride had been strenuous for him.

When the old man dismounted, Pete unsaddled
both horses to give their backs some rest and air.
Then he squatted cowboy fashion on his heels beside
Hatsy.

Down below was the glistening marvel of the
dunes. Pete could see the many hollows and ridges
which didn't seem to him to make the same kind of
sense that the canyons and gulleys on the mountain
did. Wind shaped things differently from water, he
thought.

He could see where Lost Creek disappeared into
the sand, and then out west several miles, a place
where Hatsy said it reappeared in the swamps
around a lake.

The world seemed bright and clear and wonderful, but Hatsy reminded him that they had come to

the mountain on business.

"Down there somewhere is your horse," he said. He untied the slicker from behind the cantle of his saddle, unrolled it, and took out a pair of field glasses.

Pete wondered how long he'd have to wait for his turn with the glasses, but Hatsy handed him the unopened case. "It's your horse," he said. "You find him."

The powerful lenses brought the green and white world below miles closer. Pete's eyes followed along the green as it merged with the white dunes. Maybe the horses would be grazing there in the open. All around the dunes he looked, then out onto the flat sagebrush country. Then he turned to the streams out in front and to the north. Not a horse anywhere, he thought, and wondered if he'd have to come up here day after day before getting a second glimpse of the mustangs.

Maybe an hour passed with Hatsy saying nothing much except to tell him that Hooper was the name of the dozen or so buildings which showed up in the southwest distance. Another time he identified the Happy Days mine dump a little to the north of them down on the lower slopes of Crestone Needles.

A breeze was teasing the ridges in the dunes ever so little. Just faint wisps of sand showed along their edges. Pete watched drowsily. It was hot, and he was getting sleepy with nothing to do but sit and look.

Then suddenly there was violent motion just where the dunes swung up onto the mountainside below him. He focused his binoculars, and what he saw was the wild horses.

"There they are!" he shouted and jumped, running downhill a little trying to get nearer for a better view.

"Take it easy, partner," Hatsy warned. "No man ever caught a horse by jumping around like a frog in a fire. Let's have a look.

"Something sure spooked them good," he said after a long look at the horses as they continued to fly over the soft, spongy surface of the sand. "They're headed south, too. That don't look so good." Hatsy handed the glasses back to Pete, who followed the fleeing band as they topped ridge after ridge of the dunes.

Presently Hatsy took the glasses again. "It looks like bad news," the old man said. "They're still headed south, like they sure want to get away from something. It'll take a couple of days for them to graze back anywhere near the mouth of our trap."

"Can't we ride down and start driving them back?" Pete asked.

"We might, if we had a lot of cowpokes to help us," Hatsy said. "But the only sure thing is to wait till they come back just about where we want them at the mouth of the trap."

Hatsy went on to outline in more detail than he had before the campaign for catching the horses. "We got to get between them and the dunes early some morning as they are going for water. And we need to be above them, too, in order to keep them from coming out above our trap. And we'll have to be ahead of them down by our camp. Now that's quite an order for the two of us, of which I don't aim to be one, because I've got to hide out by the box canyon."

"But that takes at least three people, and there's only me." Pete was annoyed. "I don't see how we can do it," he said.

"Take it easy. Columbus crossed the ocean, didn't he?" Hatsy replied. "Speaking of that, the great-great-granddaddies of these mustangs came over right after Columbus showed them the way. They were no-fooling Spanish horses, and they been around these dunes ever since anyone can remember. You may not get 'em in the trap on the first few tries, but they ain't going to travel back to Spain, either."

Pete was less annoyed now, but he still felt puzzled and a little hopeless. "Do you honestly think we can catch even one of them?" he asked.

"I'm not making any promises. It partly depends on luck, and I've noticed that folks who use their brains usually have the most luck."

"Well, if there's nothing to do but sit around for a couple of days," Pete said, "I guess I'd better use the time to go back to the ranch and send a letter to Mom and Dad."

"Don't forget, Clary ordered a mess of fish," said Hatsy. "Maybe we can get some before dark, and you can easy ride across to the ranch tonight. There'll be a moon."

Returning toward camp they kept up high on the mountainside. When they finally turned to drop down to camp they were above the south wing of their trap.

"When we come to our fence," Hatsy said, "you get off and make a break in the string so we can get the horses through. Even my Apaloosies will spook at those rags. When we're through you can tie the string together again and the fence'll be as good as new."

When Pete caught sight of the first fluttering rag, he dismounted and went over to the string. But he found it had been broken just where they planned to go.

"Hey, Hatsy, the fence is broken," Pete shouted in excitement.

"And Moore did it," Hatsy said, after riding up and inspecting the site. He pointed to tracks in the gravel which Pete's untrained eyes had not even noticed. "A horse and a burro have been through here, and a man with mountain boots walked around right where the break is. All adds up to say that Moore does what he pleases around here just as if he owned the whole dad-burned Sangre de Cristo range. A decent hombre would have tied that string together if he had to break it to get through. Looks like I'd better check over all our fence tomorrow morning while you're riding back here from the ranch. We could lose a lot of time if the horses found a break in the string like this and got away from us."

As Pete repaired the break he felt irritated and angry. It was beginning to look as if that queer guy Moore could be a real nuisance if he took it into his head to be one. Pete couldn't help wondering why he was so unsociable.

At camp Hatsy reached into the wagon and drew out two fishing rods, a wicker basket, and an old cigar box.

"Now don't you tromp hard when we get near where we're going, and don't you show your shadow on the water. Rainbows spook when they feel the earth shake or when they see something unusual like a cowboy from Chicago."

A little way upstream Hatsy pointed to a high bank that overhung a deep pool. Pete moved as quietly as he could and was glad he was wearing moccasins instead of high-heeled boots. Hatsy handed him a fishing pole rigged up with a big grasshopper

Pete Repaired the String Fence

already on the hook.

"I always use grasshoppers when the water's a little riled. There must have been a storm high up on Crestone Needles," Hatsy explained.

Pete looked at the water, and saw that it was not as clear as usual.

Pointing to the pool Hatsy said, "There's a big fellow hangs out here about this time of day. Just toss the line over and don't stand where he can see you or your shadow."

Down below, the water was dark under a canopy of leaves. Pete couldn't guess how Hatsy was so sure there were fish there. But he did as directed, and Hatsy went on off to another pool.

It seemed no time at all before there was a jerk on his line. He snapped the rod up as if he thought the whole world depended on him to save it that very instant.

There in the air over him he saw a flash of motion and his line followed it back into a tangle of choke-cherries.

"I got one!" he shouted and ran after it. He found his line all snarled in a bush, but no fish. He was still on his hands and knees looking for the fish among the leaves under the bush when he felt something cold go down inside his shirt collar. He jumped up and the cold thing went way down inside.

There behind him was Hatsy, cackling. In a second Pete had pulled a slippery fish from inside his shirt.

"Just happened to be going by and noticed that trout over by the big rock," Hatsy said and pointed to a boulder farther away from the creek than the bush. "First time I heard of rainbows growing out of rocks. Seems like I always had to catch mine in the water."

Pete examined his fish and saw that his excited jerk had pulled the hook right through the side of the mouth. By good luck it had fallen in a crack between two large rocks and had been wedged there firmly.

"It's the same with fishing as with horses, son," the old man said. "You don't have to do everything all at the same time and all of a sudden. And when you start something, you gotta have an idea where it's most likely to end."

Pete baited his hook again, and Hatsy showed him how to play the fighting trout until the right moment to land them. By dusk they had caught ten nice ones—just enough to make a dinner for Aunt Clara, Uncle Lem, and the hands at the ranch.

After a quick meal, Pete saddled Polkadot and started off.

Riding over the alkali flats under the moonlight, Pete was careful to keep the dunes right behind him as Hatsy had told him to do. It was easy to see the dunes each time he turned around to make sure of his bearings. They shone with an almost phosphorescent glow—a great bright heap against the darkened barrier of the mountains behind. Pete felt deep excitement as he jogged steadily toward the ranch house. Here was a world more strange and beautiful than he had ever dreamed of when he planned to spend his summer in Colorado. Each bunch of sagebrush and greasewood stood out gray and sharp in the silver light. Behind and ahead and away off to his right were the jagged, immovable mountain ranges that seemed to shut out all the hurrying, mixed-up world he had known before. Everything was perfect —the cool night breeze brushing his face as he sat relaxed, the little sounds of leather on leather that came from his saddle, the small jangle of the bit, the steady, sure beat of his horse's feet.

As he leaned in the saddle to open the last gate in the barbed-wire fence before he reached the ranch, he wished this moonlight ride didn't have to end. But there not far ahead were the outlines of the ranch buildings.

As he drew closer he saw that the one light showing came from his aunt's and uncle's bedroom. He put Polkadot in the barn where Chief woke up to greet him with a cheerful yipping and wriggling of his whole stiff old body.

"Hi, Chief, old boy," Pete said. "Getting kind of

lonesome without any horses? Here's company for
the night." He patted the dog, took his bundle of
fish from behind the cantle, and went to the kitchen.
"It's me," he called. "You needn't get up. I'll see
you in the morning."

But, as he spread his trout out in their wrappings
of damp grass on the kitchen table, Uncle Lem and
Aunt Clara came in, fully dressed.

"We thought you'd be here for supper one of
these nights," Aunt Clara said, "and we were sort of
waiting for you. It's good to see you. How's Hatsy?
Oh, Lem, look at the trout!"

"I caught three of them myself," Pete boasted.
Then he told them how Hatsy had stuffed one of
them in his shirt before he caught onto the tricks of
landing a fighting trout.

"Did you have your supper before you left camp?"
Aunt Clara asked.

"I had a mess of trout," Pete fibbed, remembering
his snack of cold beans, cold biscuits, and cold canned
tomatoes.

"You're probably starved anyway after that long
ride." Aunt Clara guessed accurately. And she set
out a big piece of apple pie, some store cheese, and a
pitcher of milk. As Pete finished his second helping
of each of these, Aunt Clara said, "You haven't had
your mail." She got a letter out of the dish cupboard,
where she always kept important papers.

"I guess I must have forgotten about it," Pete confessed. He'd been too busy thinking about how to keep from saying anything that would give away the plan he and Hatsy had for getting the horse.

He glanced hurriedly at the letter from his mother. His father was painting the house and Charlie across the street was quarantined with scarlet fever and everybody missed him. He missed his home, too, but he'd been so occupied with Hatsy that he'd forgotten all about being homesick.

"Come on, Ma, it's time to turn in," said Uncle Lem. "We can talk some more in the morning and find out what shenanigans Hatsy's up to."

But in the morning there wasn't much time, and Pete was glad of that, because he didn't want to reveal his secret. He wanted to leave right after breakfast, but Aunt Clara reminded him he should write a letter home. When this was done, he saddled up, tied on the bundle of well-wrapped, fresh-butchered beef and other treats that Uncle Lem and Aunt Clara had put together, and prepared for the ride back to camp. As he turned Polkadot east and started off at a fast walk, Old Chief panted along a little way, keeping him company.

Just before Pete reached camp, he paused at the top of a rise, hoping that he might just possibly sight the mustangs somewhere. They were not around, but off to the south something did catch his eye.

There was a man on a familiar horse. It was Moore on Bridger, and he was headed out along the flats. I wonder what that guy's up to, Pete thought, and urged Polkadot down the ridge into camp.

CHAPTER SIX

THE CHASE

By the time Pete had put the two big steaks Uncle Lem had given him into a covered pail and had weighted it down in the creek to keep cool, he heard a horse approaching. He looked up and saw Hatsy.

"That blamed coyote, Moore, busted our fence again," Hatsy fumed.

"I just saw him riding off south on Bridger," Pete replied.

"We gotta teach that guy some manners," Hatsy said, and then he added thoughtfully, "Seems to me he's doing a fair amount of riding for a man who is supposed to be taking a rest cure."

"I don't know," Pete said, "but maybe we ought to go looking for the mustangs while we know the fence is all in one piece."

"We'd just be wasting our time," Hatsy said. "You know the best time to start after them is early in the morning when they're coming for water. Then we'll have a full day ahead for working them around into the trap. I know you're anxious about them, son, but we want to do this right."

"Are we just going to sit around all day?" Pete asked, disappointed.

"It occurs to me that we might kill time by having a look at that Moore's camp and find out what kind of a housekeeper he is. I'd a little ruther pay him a social call when I'm doggone sure he's not at home."

"Do you think there's a chance of finding his camp?" Peter asked skeptically. "There's a lot of country up here."

"Remember where he broke through the south wing of the trap?" Hatsy answered. "Well, let's see if we can follow his trail back from there."

Pete was amazed at the signs that Hatsy could read as they picked up Moore's tracks at the string fence and started up the mountain. There were, of course, hoofprints here and there where the horse had crushed a scarlet Indian paintbrush to the ground. Sometimes there was nothing that Pete could see, and yet Hatsy kept on going.

"How do you know you're on the trail?" Pete asked.

"I don't always know," Hatsy said. "I just let Raindrop do the work for me a good bit of the time. Moore doesn't know this country, and he's gotta let Bridger pick his way. A good horse will find the easiest path for the most part, and that's what Raindrop is doing. Look there, now. See that rock with no lichen on it like the others. It's been turned over recently. Rocks ain't like Mexican jumping beans.

They don't turn over by themselves."

Half an hour later, Hatsy let out a snort and pointed at the ground. There was a cigarette stub lying among some rocks near a bed of dry pine needles. "Just plain fool's luck! If that hombre doesn't watch where he throws his coffin nails, he'll start a forest fire."

A few hundred yards farther, Pete yelled, "Hey! It looks like a car's been in here."

They had reached a place on the mountainside where there was a kind of shelf of grassy land that swung off to the south. There, plainly visible, were parallel lines where the rough grass had been crushed down. Only some kind of car or truck could have made those lines.

"Looks like things are going to get thicker before they get thinner," Hatsy said.

Pete grinned and they rode on, following the tracks to the left. They soon rounded the base of a ridge, and there in front of them stood two tents set in the deep shade of trees near a spring which sent a small stream tumbling off down the mountain. A loud bray from a burro tethered near by greeted them.

"It looks like we came to the right address," Pete said. "Moore keeps a neat camp, too. I wouldn't have expected it from a guy with a city hat who throws away cigarette stubs in the woods."

Hatsy nodded his head. "I'm beginning to think
there's more than bone that keeps your ears apart,
son."

They dismounted near the first of the tents and,
lifting the flap, looked in at a cot made up neatly, a
duffel bag, a folding table with tin dishes on it, a
camp chair, boxes of canned goods, and a small
canned-heat stove. Hanging from the ridgepole were
several pots and pans.

"He sure didn't pack this stuff in on a burro,"
Pete remarked. "The car that came in here must
have had quite a load."

"Let's have a look at the other tent," said Hatsy.

The other tent held only a small, sturdy table
pounded together out of planks and a heavy wooden
box with a padlock on it.

"Darndest camp setup I ever saw," said Hatsy,
"and I've seen plenty. Looks like he's living alone—
there's only one cot. So why does he need two tents
and two tables?"

"Maybe he's fixing the place up to have company
later. Let's go," Pete suggested. He'd had enough of
Moore and Moore's peculiarities. The thing that
really interested him was the mustangs and the horse
trap. Moore could live as he pleased, as long as he
quit bothering the string fence.

"Hey, wait. I've got an idea," Pete said suddenly.
"Let's leave a note telling the guy we don't care if he

goes through the string but he's got to tie it up after he's broken it. He might spoil our whole plan."

"Okay, you write it," Hatsy said.

Pete got a piece of charcoal from Moore's outdoor campfire and scrawled on the table top:

PLEASE TIE THE STRING FENCE AFTER YOU BREAK IT. THIS IS IMPORTANT. THANKS.

"I mightn't of been so polite," Hatsy remarked. "But I guess he'll get the point."

On the ride back toward camp, Pete kept looking out at the dunes wherever they showed through the trees, hoping to see the mustangs again.

"There's just a chance they'll be back around this neck of the woods early in the morning," Hatsy said at last. "After you get some chuck, you might come up long about here. You can get a good view. Bring your blankets and sleep out. Then you'll be ready to move if you should see them at daybreak. You'll be above them, so you can head them right into the trap."

When they had finished off the beefsteak and doughnuts that Aunt Clara had sent, Pete tied his roll of soogans and his slicker behind the cantle of the saddle and mounted Raindrop.

Calling out a last piece of advice, Hatsy said, "Don't make a fire. That might send the mustangs clear across the dunes. Take it easy going up the hill

Pete Scrawled a Note on the Tabletop

now. I'll go up the box canyon tomorrow, just on the chance you have some luck."

It was moonlight before Pete reached the point above the dunes where he could watch for the horses. There, as he munched a cold biscuit, he looked over the great mysterious waste. A brisk wind was stirring the dunes into life, and a low steady moan came from the sand as the wind took up its endless work of shifting it from one place to another and then back again.

Along the crests, sand waved in the wind like the manes and tails of huge horses. Pete could see how the old legend got started about the giant web-footed animals racing there on moonlight nights. But tonight there really might be horses out there, if he could only see them. And in the morning, perhaps he would be racing them.

A coyote howled. Its lonesome wail made Pete feel more alone and far away than he had thought anyone could ever feel. He had heard coyotes before back on the ranch and in camp with Hatsy, but then it was different. Hatsy had snorted in disgust when the long sliding cry had broken the night. "Lotta noise, little wit!" he grumbled. "Often wonder what those cowardly sneaks think they're scaring with their racket. Everybody knows they wouldn't jump anything with more fight in it than a lamb."

But there the cry was, and it sent shivers down Pete's back. He lay down in his blankets with Raindrop tethered close by. But he could not sleep. A rabbit thumping along startled the horse who snorted and stomped his ironclad feet in the coarse gravel. Little strange noises near by kept breaking through the steady moan of the dunes, but finally Pete dozed off.

When he woke it was pitch black. The moon was gone and he was stiff and chilly. For a minute he couldn't even see Raindrop, standing asleep there, but soon his eyes made out his light hindquarters, and Pete somehow felt reassured. He shivered and turned over, with his face out toward the valley where he knew he woud see the first slanting rays of dawn.

When dawn did come, it first lit a peak in the San Juan mountains which made the western wall around the San Luis Valley. Then, so fast you could see the light driving the darkness before it, the night fled down the mountains and eastward across the valley floor. Almost before he could roll his blankets and get the saddle on Raindrop, sunlight had spilled down onto the dunes. And there, close enough for a good look, were the beautiful young stallion and about twenty other mustangs walking warily across the sand in the direction of the creek—just as Hatsy had predicted.

Pete was downwind from the horses, and the moan of the dunes and the squeaking of the sand under their big hoofs would keep them from noticing him, he hoped. He rode down toward the dunes, keeping behind a ridge out of sight of the band as it moved nervously toward water. Twice he caught a glimpse of them, trotting along ahead, off the dunes now, just where he wanted them. If they kept on in that direction, he would soon be able to head them into the trap.

Raindrop slipped and skidded as he struggled up a steep slope in the sand until he finally got steady footing on a ridge. There ahead went the mustangs. Leading the mares and colts was the old stallion, and close by the young stallion trotted with swift, sure motions. Pete liked the spirited way he held his handsome head as he paused occasionally to glance around. This would be a mount to be proud of. Pete was determined to get him for his own. Maybe even today.

But the sight of the mustangs was too much for Raindrop. He whinnied. The wild horses turned in interest, then seeing Pete astride Raindrop, they loped off toward the woods and the creek. Pete dropped back down behind the ridge, urged Raindrop off the dunes as fast as his small feet would carry him, and turned up into the woods behind the band. There, over the rough ground he made as good time as he could. But the horses were keeping a sharp lookout for him. The stallion in the lead stopped every once in a while and looked back at the dunes.

So far everything was going according to plan. But now came the biggest job of all. Pete had to turn the mustangs toward the trap. The danger was that they would get too far ahead and dash back into the sand. Pete had to close the distance between himself and the herd. Raindrop picked his way carefully down a steep slope and broke into a gallop. Pete tried to urge him ahead faster. The mustangs were out of sight now among the cottonwoods and willows along the creek.

Maybe Pete could keep up with them and stay on their left, frightening them away from the dunes. As he climbed another ridge he caught sight of the band again. There, almost a quarter of a mile ahead, they stood poised, as if undecided whether they were still being followed, and, if so, which way to run. Pete drove Raindrop on. He had to turn the band. Throwing caution to the winds he waved his hat frantically. But he was too late.

The band broke and ran with incredible speed—right back toward the dunes. They were there in a second, and they did not seem to slow up as soft sand replaced hard mountain earth and rocks beneath their hoofs. Raindrop hadn't a chance in the world of turning them now.

With a feeling of utter dismay, Pete watched them

disappear into the dunes. It might be days now before he would have another chance as good. The mustangs had sought protection in the sand where they alone could go with ease. Pete had lost the race.

CHAPTER SEVEN

THE YOUNG STALLION

Thoughtfully, Pete rode back to camp. How in the world could he, singlehanded, keep the mustangs from turning back into the sand? If he could stay out on the dunes, and if he had a horse that could race on the sand as fast as the mustangs could on the hard earth, he might do it. But that was impossible. Nor was it possible to extend the trap farther. It would take weeks of work to cut and carry all the stakes needed to set up a string fence on the sand. Maybe he just couldn't do the job alone. Perhaps he'd have to ask help from the ranch. Even Aunt Clara could do the trick, standing at the right place and waving her apron.

Pete shook his head. He wasn't going to let anyone at the ranch know about all this. Then suddenly he had an idea. What about Old Chief? The dog couldn't run, but he could bark. And he'd be certain to bark if he saw a band of horses racing toward him. Maybe if Pete stationed Old Chief just at the place where the horses had escaped today, the dog would turn them back, straight into the trap. He decided it was worth trying.

Briskly now, Pete unsaddled Raindrop and tethered the weary horse where he could graze. Then, filling his pockets with raisins and cold biscuits, he set off on foot to find Hatsy who he was sure would be waiting at the box canyon.

"Hatsy!" Pete called as he approached the gate.

"Fine sight you are," Hatsy called back, coming out from the chokecherry bush beside the gate. "You go off on my Apaloosie to bring in a bunch of mustangs, and you come back afoot. What's the matter—those wild horses spook you?"

Pete explained what had happened, as the old man squatted down crosslegged and resumed work on a pair of new moccasins he'd brought along to make while he was waiting. Then Pete told his idea about Old Chief.

"Might be worth trying," Hatsy said. "But what you going to tell Lem and Clary?"

"I'll figure out something," Pete replied. "Can I borrow Polkadot and start right now? We ought to let Raindrop rest today. You can ride back to camp and I'll climb aboard there."

Hatsy agreed, and by early afternoon Pete was back at the ranch again.

"I declare!" Aunt Clara exclaimed. "I didn't expect to see you so soon. Anything wrong?"

Pete tried his best to look serious as he told the story he'd made up. "Hatsy asked me to do a chore last night and I forgot. Now we're in a jam. He told me to put both the saddles in the wagon where they'd be up out of reach of skunks. It slipped my mind, and so this morning we found that skunks had been eating the latigo straps. They chewed them off the cinches on both saddles and ate them up or dragged them away or something. Hatsy only had one spare strap in the wagon, so that means we can only ride one horse at a time. I thought maybe I could borrow a couple of new ones from Uncle Lem."

Aunt Clara scolded him a little for his carelessness while she warmed up a meal for him. Uncle Lem came in presently, and Pete repeated the tale.

"You're not the first cowboy who's been set afoot by a skunk," Uncle Lem said. "There's something special about latigo straps that the varmints just can't stay away from. I'll get you a couple of extras from the shed."

While Uncle Lem was digging out the straps, Pete told him there was something else he'd like to have. He'd like to borrow Old Chief, just in case he forgot about the saddles again. Uncle Lem looked at Pete for a minute. Then he grinned a little as if he'd been told the moon was made of green cheese. But he said only, "If it's all right with Clara, I guess you can."

Aunt Clara agreed to the proposal. "It does anybody good to get a little mountain air," she said. "But if you bring that dog back smelling of skunk,

I'll make you sleep out on the range the rest of the summer."

"How you going to carry him?" Uncle Lem asked. "He hasn't walked seven miles in the last ten years."

"He's small, even if he is fat," Pete said. "I could carry him in front of me on the saddle in that big grape basket hanging in the shed."

At first Old Chief wasn't very happy in the basket. But the rhythmic motion of Polkadot's slow walk made him doze off after a while. By sundown Pete and Chief arrived at camp. Pete's own empty stomach reminded him with a sudden jolt that he'd not considered how they'd feed the dog. He confessed his worry to Hatsy who was fussing around the Dutch oven near the fire.

"There's enough rabbit here in the pot for the three of us—providing you don't make a pig of yourself," the old man said.

"How did you get a rabbit?" Pete asked.

"Same way anybody gets a rabbit without shooting it," Hatsy replied. "I caught it in a snare. It's all good eating, too. You don't have to worry about picking buckshot out of your teeth. Chief will make out all right. You don't have to fear about that."

Confidently Pete set off on Raindrop after supper. Hatsy agreed to take Chief out on the dunes at the first light of dawn and tie him there. He'd drag a log out at the same time, big enough so Chief couldn't

Old Chief Rode Back With Pete

get away. If Pete missed the horses, he would bring Chief back to camp with him. In any case, it wouldn't hurt the dog to spend a few hours by himself on the warm sand. It didn't get uncomfortably hot till midday, and by that time they'd be sure to come and get him.

But for the next three days, Pete didn't even catch a glimpse of the horses coming out of the sand for their early morning drink. The second and third day he stayed high on the mountainside and caught sight of them far out in the dunes. They were huddled with their heads drooped.

"I've never seen such goings on," Hatsy said finally when Pete brought Chief back into camp. "Those mustangs can't be getting much grass— they're out there on the sand so much. But they'll be losing strength, and they should be easier to round up when you do get a chance. Something has sure spooked them. But I don't think we did all of it. We've been mighty quiet. Something else scared 'em."

On the fourth morning, Pete was patiently watching at the same point where he'd spent the first night. As day began to reach down the mountainside below him, he saw some motion in the dim light along the edge of the dunes. In a moment he realized that here were his mustangs, seeking a watering place.

Tense with excitement, Pete urged Raindrop down the slope. He could not fail now. Just as he had done the first time, he outflanked the horses, first getting behind them on the dunes, then circling above them, and then following them down toward the creek.

The horses moved more slowly than before, Pete thought. His stallion was there, and he seemed fresher than any of the others. The lead stallion did not even turn to look back, but kept on doggedly toward the creek.

Now Pete urged Raindrop down off the dunes onto hard ground, too. With Old Chief waiting out in the sand, he could make a bold dash up behind the herd. As the thirsty animals plunged ankle deep into the creek and began to drink, Pete put Raindrop into a gallop, and waving his slicker, he charged right down toward them. Instantly, fear overcame thirst, and the mustangs turned back toward the protecting dunes.

And then Old Chief's bark came from one of the first ridges in the dunes. Pete could hear his yapping above the moaning of the sand. At the top of a ridge the horses stopped. They milled and hesitated. Chief was doing just what Pete had expected. Suddenly the old stallion turned and led the herd directly into the mouth of the funnel.

For the moment, Pete had them exactly where he

wanted them. His only job was to keep them traveling on into the funnel. If they swerved either to right
or left, they would run into the string fence, and, by
staying below them, he could push them on toward
the box canyon. The only danger was that they might
turn and run straight back for the dunes.

Pete remembered where the fence was and gauged
his position carefully. Although he kept behind and
below the mustangs, the lead stallion suddenly
swung in almost a half circle and made a break toward open country. Pete used his spurs on Raindrop
for the first time, forcing the horse at a full gallop up
across the rough ground which lay between him and
the string fence. He had to turn those mustangs.

In a moment he knew he'd done it. He eased up
on Raindrop as the mustangs swung a little to the
right, which brought them closer to the string fence.
Pete was near enough to see what happened when
they charged toward the fluttering colored rags. The
lead stallion pulled up short, reared back, and
snorted. The young stallion, the mares, and colts
milled in a frenzy of confusion before the unexpected barrier. Then they turned back into the canyon, heading into the trap.

The ground here was rough and covered with
brush, making it difficult for the band to keep close
together. The young stallion was to the left, with
several mares pushing along near him. Suddenly, as

if he sensed the trap, the old stallion darted sharply to the right. Most of the mares followed him. Before the young stallion and the mares near him sensed the change in direction, Pete spurred Raindrop in between the two groups of mustangs. Swinging his slicker, he frightened the smaller group, led by the young stallion, straight on, nearer the box canyon. Pete no longer cared about the large group. The horse he wanted was still ahead, running into the trap.

The north bank of the creek had less underbrush, and the horses raced along there as best they could. Then they cut sharply to the left and up toward higher, freer ground. Pete could not head them off here. He could only hope that the string fence worked. He kept his panting horse behind and below, while the mustangs headed up the hill. In no time there was a sharp whinny of fear, as the mustangs saw another fluttering line of rags ahead. They swerved again, thundering along inside the string with its bright-colored bits of cloth.

On and on the horses went, splashing down into the creek and across. Pete still came at them from below. The mouth of the funnel was narrowing. It was now or never. One lunge through that string and the whole chase would be spoiled. Pete moved as steadily behind the band as he could but kept well back to be ready to head them off if they turned.

At the entrance to the box canyon they hesitated.
The young stallion looked back. There on either
side were the lines of fluttering rags. And between
them rode Pete waving his slicker, heading off any
retreat. The stallion turned and fled into the corral,
with three mares close behind him.

Now Pete saw the top bar of the corral slide into
position. Hatsy had done his part of the job. The
rest of the mares came to a frightened, panting halt
in front of the bar. Pete reined and turned to the left
behind them, as Hatsy slipped the other two bars
into place.

A moment later, Hatsy stepped from behind the
chokecherry bush, swung his sombrero, and started

the free mustangs back down the canyon toward the sand dunes. It was a lucky break that only four had entered the small corral before Hatsy closed it off.

Pete turned Raindrop for a moment back down the canyon, shouted, and waved his slicker to make sure the mares were on their way to rejoin the band on the dunes. Then he rode to the corral and jumped off to join Hatsy who was watching the wild-eyed, frightened creatures inside the gate.

Pete was interested only in the young stallion who moved nervously about, his chest heaving, his sides flecked with foam. The mares just stood with their heads down, panting, feet spread.

Hatsy swung up to the top rail of the gate, rope in

hand. "Quick, son," he said. "See if you can dab your rope on the stallion's head. Make your cast from on top of that rock over on the left, and be careful to snub around a tree. Otherwise you'll get pulled down into the corral. I'll make another cast from the gate here and snub around a gatepost. We want to make sure he doesn't get away when we turn the mares loose."

It was easy enough for Pete just to drop his loop over the mustang's head. But the horse reared with such sudden terror, when he felt the rope strike his neck and then tighten, that Pete was nearly jerked off the rock before he got the rope snubbed. As the rope slid through his bare hands, Pete made a lunge sideways and brought the rope across the trunk of the tree he had planned to snub on. The added friction on the rope gave him the help he needed. Now he could stand there ready to let it out or take it up as Hatsy directed.

Hatsy crawled through the gate bars and Pete saw him build a loop and just hold it quietly at his side. Then in a flash as the horse reared back in his struggle against the rope on his neck, Hatsy swung the lariat low from the ground and caught the horse's two front feet. In no time Hatsy was back through the bars, and the stallion was securely caught by both his neck and forefeet. The two ropes pulled him and held him close to one side of the corral. He stood there, helpless, quivering.

The mares milled in terror over on the far side of the corral. Hatsy tied his rope, then pulled out the bars of the gate and called to Pete to haze the mares out of the corral. Pete made his rope fast and scrambled around the rim of rocks to where the mares stood below him. He waved his hat. This new frightening motion sent the mares streaming out the gate and down the hill toward the sand dunes, and safety.

Hatsy replaced the bars. "Now we're going to ease up on our ropes. Give the horse plenty of slack," he called.

Pete did as he was told. In a second the stallion was free and had fled to the far side of the corral away from his captors. Pete and Hatsy leaned on the bars and looked at the magnificent animal.

"You've got a good horse," Hatsy said. "And you did a good job getting him."

Pete didn't answer. He was tired, and happier than he had ever been in his life.

CHAPTER EIGHT

SANDY GETS HIS NAME

"Have you thought what you're going to call him?" Hatsy asked.

"Sure. I've had a lot of time to think these last few days," Pete replied. "He's mostly the color those dunes are sometimes, and he came from the dunes. His name's going to be Sandy."

"Okay. Now you've got him, what are you going to do with him?" the old man asked impishly.

"First thing I'm going to do is let him cool off," Pete replied. "He's thirsty, but I'm going to give him a good rest before he has a drink."

"Given any thought as to how he's going to get water? He's in the corral and there's no water there. If you let him out, you can have the fun of chasing him again. And next time he won't stop this side of the Mexican border."

Here was a stumper. Pete *hadn't* thought how he was going to water the wild horse while he was shut up in the corral.

"Well, I'll give you a hand this time," Hatsy said. "But from now till you graduate, you gotta do the rest of your homework yourself. He's your horse and you'll have to take care of him."

Pete looked the corral over more carefully than he had before. There was some grass inside, but after it was gone how was he going to feed Sandy? He hadn't thought that one out either.

"What are we going to do for feed?" Pete said guiltily.

"You might share your cornflakes with him," Hatsy said with a grin.

"We can't let him out to pasture," Pete thought out loud. "He's not broke even to lead on a tether rope. We'd have an awful time getting hobbles on him right now."

"So what are you going to do?" Hatsy asked.

"I guess I'll have to bring him food," Pete decided. "Can we get some hay at the ranch?"

"There's some hay in my wagon," Hatsy confessed. "I brought a bale along just in case."

"Well, let's get it," Pete said eagerly.

"Hold on," Hatsy said. "He won't starve in there. Let him rest, get some grass. That's what he's used to, anyway. Later on we can see about hay."

Hatsy paused, then went on. "I'm going down now to get Old Chief. He'll be pretty thirsty and tired out there on the sand. I'll bring up my bedroll and some chuck. You go get your roll where you left it on the mountain. We're camping here tonight. Tomorrow we'll bring up the wagon and make our permanent camp near the corral. It does a new horse good to have friends around. It does any horse good."

Hatsy rode off on Polkadot who had been care-fully tethered away from the stream so he had not had a drink all day. "Don't you water Raindrop till I get back," the old man called over his shoulder. Pete wondered about this but asked no questions at the time. He had too many other things on his mind.

A couple of hours later Pete rode in with his soo-gans, and not long afterward Hatsy came back up the trail, with his bedroll behind the cantle of his saddle. Pushing slowly along behind him was Old Chief. When the dog saw Pete he gave a tired but cheerful bark of recognition, and then just dropped down in the grass panting.

"How's the fine stallion?" Hatsy asked. "Been eat-ing any grass yet?"

Pete who had been hanging over the bars of the gate watching Sandy with pride and fascination, an-swered, "Yes, he's been nibbling for a while."

"He'll be ready for water then," Hatsy said. He brought both the Apaloosas up close to the gate, hob-bled them, and took off their saddles. Then the old man produced three buckets he had hidden in the bushes. Pete filled them at the stream. He carried one for each of the Apaloosas and placed the third inside the corral. The Apaloosas sloshed the water down their dry throats. It wasn't long before Sandy, imitating the other horses, and being famished for water himself, moved cautiously toward the bucket which was near the gate—and the other horses. He was soon taking his water in great gulps.

"That's the way we're going to gentle Sandy," Hatsy said. "He can learn a lot by copying the Apaloosies. None of the rough stuff for us. I couldn't ride a bucking bronc anyway and you're not going to try."

Hatsy went downwind from the corral and out of sight. There he built a fire over which to prepare chuck for the two of them. All the time he was busy with his cooking Pete hung over the rails of the corral gate and talked to his horse in a low tone of voice with every sound of friendliness he could put into his words.

"Sandy, you're my horse. You're mine. You're going to be such a good horse no one will ever notice your feet are oversize. You don't need to be scared of Old Chief here. He barks sometimes but he's a good dog with horses. Sandy, you're my horse."

"You sure have a good feel for horses, son," the old man said quietly as he came close to the corral. "But don't talk too much. It might make the animal nervous. It doesn't do any horse good to have a whole gabfest going on around him all the time. Another thing, when you start to gentle him never make a quick move. Slow and easy. You'll have that horse eating out of your hand before long. Did you bring any sugar?"

"No, I didn't. I never thought of that."

"I didn't either," the old man said, "because it ain't needed. We won't need any sugar to do the job. But every now and then a little tidbit won't hurt at all."

Tired though he was, Sandy stomped and snorted and sniffed in the corral all night long. In the morning he watched with bright, attentive eyes the saddling of the two Apaloosas, as Hatsy and Pete prepared to go down and get the wagon.

It was a tricky job to maneuver the wagon through the rough country where no road led, but Hatsy managed it expertly. A few times Pete had to get out and chop down small aspens that blocked the way. At last they clattered across the creek and up into the little park at the corral. Their arrival excited Sandy who plunged from one side to another of his small enclosure. His proud head was up and his tail spiked as he made his short dashes back and forth. The excitement of watching the men unpack kept Sandy nervous and edgy as the morning wore on.

He jumped when Pete rattled the pothooks and the Dutch oven that he set down at the spot where they had decided to have their campfire.

"Shall I take out the hay?" Pete called from the wagon.

"No, leave it there to keep dry," Hatsy answered. "When Sandy's used up all the grass, we'll give him a lesson in table manners."

Then Hatsy explained his plan. They would teth-er the Apaloosas just outside the corral gate and let them eat off the grass there first, as Sandy was grazing inside. Then, when they all needed a good meal, Pete and Hatsy would throw down hay.

"One thing a horse has is a good memory," Hatsy said. "He'll remember that other horses eat hay and that hay is good and that you and I give hay to horses when they are hungry."

As the unpacking went on, Raindrop and Polka-dot grazed near the gate. Once in a while they put their long, dark necks curiously over the top bar and looked at Sandy. He danced a little, trotted back and forth, and looked toward them with obvious interest.

At last, Pete walked quietly to the corral and stood beside the Apaloosas. Sandy watched him—and kept his distance. Pete looked at his horse's well-muscled shoulders and strong thighs. "You've got what it takes," he said. "You'll be a strong running horse. You're going to be a good all-round cow horse. So good that I can work next summer as a regular cow-hand."

The following day, Pete spent some time putting a braided hackamore on Polkadot's head, then taking it off and letting the Apaloosa snuggle up to him. Next he put the hackamore on Raindrop, took it off, and patted that horse's beautiful dark cheek. Toward the end of the afternoon, Sandy was more and more curious, and less and less afraid to stand near the gate. Finally he put his head across the bars, so close that Pete could touch him.

Pete's hand shot up to stroke the sculptured neck. But the quick movement sent Sandy racing to the back of the corral in fear. Pete was angry with himself. "I wonder if I'll ever learn to do things gradually instead of all of a sudden," he thought. "It'll take him a while to get that close again."

Later, Hatsy told Pete to go and practice with his rope a little way off from the corral so as not to frighten Sandy. Pete spent his time making easy throws out onto a patch of grass. No big swings, no fancy casts at first. Next day Hatsy said, "Now try casts at this old tree stump. Just dab your noose on that post about a thousand times from different distances."

Pete went eagerly to work at first, learning the ways of his rope. But then the monotony of the routine began to bore him. Constant repetition of the same thing was just too much. Pete threw his rope down impatiently and went over to the corral, wishing he could get on Sandy right now and ride off.

"Trouble with you is you want to be someplace without bothering to get there," Hatsy said cheerfully. "Looks like somebody's got to gentle you before you can gentle your horse."

The Quick Movement Startled Sandy

Pete was too annoyed to answer, but he halfway suspected that Hatsy was right. Still, that didn't make him like it.

When he had calmed down a little, Hatsy said, "Okay, next thing on the menu is roping the Apaloosies."

This was a change, at least, and Pete welcomed it. He took the hobbles off Raindrop and cast his rope with all the strength of his arm. This was more like it. The loop sailed through the air—high and beyond Raindrop's head.

Pete looked around at Hatsy, and, before the old man could say a word, Pete remarked, "I know I was too anxious. It's going to be right next time." And it was.

He took turns roping first Raindrop, then Polkadot. This went on for some time, the Apaloosas showing no fright. They had been trained early to respond to the rope and had never feared it.

Often during the next days Hatsy talked to Pete about gentling horses. He had no truck with the theory that they should be broken in a day. He did not want to have the spirit ruined in any horse he handled.

"They say mine is a soft Eastern way," Hatsy pointed out. "They say it makes one-man horses. I say it's a good way, and it's a poor specimen of a man who can't handle a horse I've gentled. I like a horse to keep his spirit, and Sandy there has lots of spirit. He showed that the minute he came in here."

Pete looked at Sandy and saw that he was as lively as any horse could be. He was fresh and rested now, and well filled-out. Somehow Pete felt that his prancing from one side of the corral to the other was as much for delight in living as it was from desire to be back with the other mustangs. Sandy seemed to be enjoying it where he was.

CHAPTER NINE

"TAKE IT EASY!"

One morning Hatsy said, "Pete, it looks like the pack rats have been getting at our grub—the ones from Chicago, I mean. And that dog hasn't been easy on our chuck either. I'm going to take Chief back to the ranch today with the wagon and pick up some more hay and anything in the line of food for us that Clary can spare. All we got left is some cinnamon, the makings of some biscuits and enough bacon fat to fry yourself a couple of messes of trout. But you'll have to catch 'em. I'll be back before noon tomorrow."

As Hatsy hitched up the team he added, "If you've got any extra time on your hands you might roll up Clary's string. No use leaving it around to mess up the mountainside and spook our own horses. Besides, we don't want to run the risk of having those sand dune mustangs accidentally wander up into the trap and come near enough to Sandy to get him excited again."

When Hatsy and Chief had gone, Pete decided his first job was to get some fish. He didn't want to live on biscuits alone until Hatsy returned. The fishing was not as good this morning as it had been on the day he had first tried it, but he persisted and by noon had a mess big enough to last him for two or three meals.

All afternoon he trudged along the fence rolling up string and stuffing it with the rags into a gunny sack. He started at the far end of the south line and worked toward camp. Part way back he found a break just where Moore's first break had been. Fresh horse tracks made Pete sure that Moore had gone over the same trail again. Although Pete no longer needed the trap, he was angry at Moore for continuing to destroy it. It looked as if that queer stranger just wanted to be annoying.

By the time he got back to the corral, the big sack of string and rags was very heavy and awkward to carry. Pete was tired, and he flopped down on the grass by the corral gate to rest. He enjoyed the horsy smell that came from the corral as he relaxed on the soft mattress of grass. He felt drowsy and soon dropped off into a nap.

A sudden snort from Sandy aroused him. By the time Pete got to his feet he saw the horse was obviously scared of something. Sandy reared and turned, rushing back and forth along one side of the small enclosure. Whatever had disturbed him must be on the other side, or above the corral in the brush and rocks.

Pete could see nothing. He thought maybe a rat-

tlesnake had come out on the warm rocks. He knew
horses were easily spooked by rattlers. But he
couldn't see one anywhere. There was no calming
Sandy, so Pete decided he had better have a look
around.

He climbed up on the rocks above the corral and
looked around. There didn't seem to be anything
there to frighten a horse. "Perhaps there's something
farther in the brush," he thought, and he started up
the slope. Through the trees he saw a movement just
ahead. There was Moore mounting Bridger and
lighting out at a fast trot.

Pete shouted, but Moore gave no sign he had
heard except to urge his horse on faster. There was
no hope of catching him on foot, Pete thought. And
what would he do if he did catch him? Moore was
husky—and mean.

As Pete turned back down the mountainside to
the corral, he felt uneasy.

"It gives you the creeps," he thought, "to have
somebody spying on you while you're asleep." Even
if Moore had visited the camp simply from curiosity,
Pete didn't like the idea. It would have been different if the guy had called out and said whatever was
on his mind.

At the corral Pete looked around for any signs of
what Moore might have been doing. He could find
nothing. Apparently Sandy's fright or Pete's own

appearance when he woke up had decided Moore to turn around and leave.

Sandy was still nervous, and Pete got water and hay for him. Then he leaned over the corral gate and talked as soothingly as he could while the horse suspiciously held aloof.

It was a long time before Sandy came for a drink and began to nibble cautiously at his hay. While he ate, Pete just stayed motionless and silent on the gate. When the horse had finished, he began his soothing talk again, then moved away to prepare his supper.

As trout sizzled in the frying pan, he made up his mind to sleep close to the corral tonight. Sandy's keen ears and nose would tell him if someone was approaching. Besides it was just one more way of getting Sandy used to having him around.

After his strenuous day he didn't lie awake long worrying about a possible visit in the night, and he didn't wake up until it was broad daylight. Apparently nothing had happened while he slept, and there was Sandy as calm as could be, just switching his tail and looking at him curiously.

Pete brought a bucket of water from the creek and shoved it under the gate. Then he leaned over the top bar. Sandy gave a sniff of interest and pranced a little at the rear of the corral. Then he trotted over to the bucket.

As he lowered his head to drink, Pete talked quietly to him.

Sandy was near enough to touch, but Pete waited until the horse had satisfied his thirst. Sandy gave a last snuffle at the bucket, lifted his head, and stood there calmly with no sign of uneasiness at being so close to Pete.

Slowly Pete reached out his big hand and laid the palm of it firmly against the tawny cheek of the stallion. Instead of jumping away, Sandy returned the pressure. Pete stroked the horse's cheek a time or two and then climbed down off the rail. Because of his excitement, he knew he'd better not run the risk of spoiling things. He felt like prancing, himself, but he simply turned and walked quietly away from the corral.

About noon Hatsy's wagon rumbled across the creek into camp.

"Hi, pardner," he called cheerily. "Did you leave any fish in the creek?"

"There are a few small ones for you." Pete grinned back at him.

"Here, you unload the wagon," Hatsy directed. "Clary sent some pie and stuff that's got to be et up in a hurry. I'll get it ready."

Pete waited until they were eating to boast. "I did it this morning," he said. "I stroked Sandy's face and he didn't jump away. I wasn't too quick this time, and I bet he'll let me do it again."

"That's a good job," Hatsy said. "I guess it's about time for you to go right into the corral."

In his eagerness to tell about Sandy, Pete had almost forgotten the news about Moore. When Hatsy heard the story, he said, "Looks like that hombre is moseying around trying to find something to keep him busy. Well, we got more important things to think about. Go into the corral now and move quietly around. Remember, Sandy's watching everything you do. You're a strange animal to him, and he's got to take his own time finding out you don't mean danger. The more things he sees you do and gets used to, the better. I'll be here with my rope in case he gets excited and tries any funny business."

Pete's heart pounded as he climbed through the gate bars. This was a big moment he'd been waiting for. He and his own horse would be together and not kept apart by a fence. He stood quietly inside the corral, talking softly. "Sandy, don't worry. I'm your friend."

The horse shook his head, pranced around, and moved excitedly back and forth in the deep end of the little box canyon—always keeping his alert eyes on Pete.

Pete walked slowly to the snubbing post and leaned against it. Sandy trotted around him once in a big circle, then stopped and gave an appraising look at the intruder. Pete squatted down. He picked up a twig and began to make aimless doodles in the earth, keeping one eye on his horse. Finally, Sandy seemed to lose interest and began to nibble at some blades of grass. Pete got up and walked quietly to the edge of the corral and back to the snubbing post. Later he picked up the water bucket and shoved it through the bars. He removed his hat and put it back on, thinking of motions that Sandy would have to get used to.

"Okay now," Hatsy finally said. "Get your lariat and prove you're as good as I think you are. Get in there with Sandy and try it on him a few times. Remember I'll be here with my rope."

Pete entered the corral and began maneuvering, with his rope hanging quietly at his side. Then he showed the rope to Sandy and made a few low swings with it. He tossed it over the snubbing post. Sandy was startled at the quick motion required for the throw. But nothing had happened to him. Pete made more casts at the snubbing post and then at the gateposts. He kept this up until Sandy had quieted down. Then Pete surprised Hatsy by leaving the corral and roping Raindrop two or three times.

"Smarter'n I figured you were," Hatsy said with real appreciation in his voice as Pete climbed back into the corral.

Pete Tossed His Rope Over the Snubbing Post

"I just want to make a few more casts in the corral," Pete said. "Tomorrow I'll try roping him."

"And we're going to spend the rest of the afternoon hazing us some trout upstream," Hatsy replied.

As they worked upstream, casting in the pools and ripples, Pete had only part of his mind on fishing. Much of the time he was thinking of his horse and planning the next steps he would take to win his confidence. Once in a while his mind wandered to Moore, and he looked for any signs that the man had been along this section of the stream which he and Hatsy hadn't yet explored. But look as he would, he could find nothing to show that Moore had been around.

When Pete dropped the one trout he had caught into the basket on top of three Hatsy already had there, the old man said, "You got to pay as much attention to catching fish as you do to gentling horses, but we got enough for one meal, so let's call it a day."

Next morning Pete roped the two Apaloosas once each, as they stood close to the corral gate. Each time he swung the loop up from his side instead of swinging it over his head as he had done before. Then talking quietly he went into the corral, and, using the same kind of toss, put the rope on Sandy's head. The mustang reared back, with a startled snort, and began to run.

In a sudden panic, Pete realized he'd been in such a hurry that he'd overlooked one thing. He'd forgotten to stand close enough to the snubbing post. Now he couldn't pass the rope around it in order to get a better hold.

The frightened stallion jerked. The rope slid painfully across Pete's bare hands and whipped back and forth across the ground as Sandy dashed around the edge of the corral. Pete jumped after the rope. His sudden leaps sent a new wave of fear through Sandy. The horse reared and his flailing front feet tangled with the rope. Then he came down, shaking his head. The loop opened up, and one enormous toss of his head sent the lariat flying off and to the ground.

Sandy was free of the troublesome rope now. Pete recovered it and crawled out through the bars. He turned his back to Hatsy, coiled the lariat, and stood leaning on the gate. The old man said nothing at all.

Toward the end of the afternoon, Sandy had calmed down completely. Pete re-entered the corral and this time stood close to the snubbing post. His cast was a good one and he snubbed fast. The rope held firm around the post as Sandy reared back against it. Pete let the horse feel the rope for a few seconds, then loosened it quickly from the post and gave it a flip. This sent a wave along the rope, opening the loop. Sandy shook his head free.

Pete waited a while before he made another cast. This time he let the rope stay on a little longer. After the fourth time, Sandy seemed much less frightened, and Pete decided he'd had enough for now. Leaving the corral, he roped first Raindrop and then Polkadot in full view of the corral. Instead of flipping the loop off their heads, he walked toward each horse while still holding the rope, using a hand-over-hand motion.

Then he tried the same thing with Sandy. Instead of being scared, Sandy seemed to enter into the spirit of the thing. He didn't resist the rope, but moved toward Pete, thus keeping the rope slack, and he seemed to wait for an approving pat when Pete loosened the honda each time.

As Pete took the rope off for the last time that afternoon, he gave Sandy his first delicacy—half of one of the apples that Aunt Clara had put in the wagon. Sandy sniffed at it, tried it out gingerly in his mouth. The apple passed inspection. It disappeared. Apparently well-pleased with himself, Sandy switched his tail and trotted around the corral with his head held high.

Holding the other half of the apple in reserve, Pete got Sandy used to feeling the hackamore on his head that evening after supper. With this new experiment, as with the others, Sandy seemed to show a cautious curiosity rather than fear. And he seemed to find reassurance in having the Apaloosas near, along with the old man and the boy.

CHAPTER TEN

SACKING OUT

For some time now Pete and Hatsy had spent most of their mornings at the corral with Sandy and the afternoons fishing. Pete wanted a change from the routine.

"Mind if I give Polkadot some exercise this afternoon and ride along the edge of the dunes and do a little exploring?" Pete said to Hatsy. "I was mostly in a kind of hurry when I was down there chasing the horses."

"The Chicago end of this creek seems to be kind of fished out, so go ahead," Hatsy replied. "But wait until you've got Sandy ready to ride before you go out into the dunes."

Without waiting for lunch, Pete rolled up some cold biscuits, cheese, and apples in his slicker, tied the bundle behind the cantle and set off.

Polkadot had done nothing but eat and rest for several days. He was frisky and fun to ride. As he reached the upper edge of the dunes Pete let him break into a lope a couple of times where the ground was smooth enough. Occasionally he had the horse walk on the dunes, but the squeak and scrunch of the sand under his hoofs bothered Polkadot. He seemed to dislike the sliding, uncertain, noisy stuff, so Pete rode mainly on solid ground.

He studied the way the purple and brown shadows in the hollows of the sand rose perceptibly as the sun dropped down in the sky. The afternoon was wearing on, and Pete suddenly realized that he'd been too interested in other things to remember about his lunch. Still, he didn't want to dismount and eat. Instead, he knotted the ends of the reins and looped them over the saddlehorn. Then, as Polkadot walked on, Pete turned in the saddle and untied one end of the rolled-up slicker. As he was reaching for the other end, he heard a burst of sound in the brush ahead. Polkadot stopped. Pete looked up and around.

There ahead a small fawn was bouncing away stiff-legged. A bit of open ground lay between Pete and the fawn. On a sudden impulse, he touched Polkadot with his heels and began to chase the little creature at full gallop. The fawn dodged first one way, then another in confusion. It occurred to Pete he might even rope it.

The chase brought out the cow pony in Polkadot. This fawn was the same as a calf to him, and he followed it skillfully as it dodged. Pete started to unlimber his rope. In the instant he looked down at his loop, Polkadot swerved after the fleeing fawn, straight under a big aspen. The next thing Pete knew, he was on the ground with the breath knocked out of him. A limb of the aspen had swept him from the saddle. Ahead, Polkadot still raced on. Why didn't he stop? Then Pete knew. He had knotted the reins around the saddlehorn when he turned to get his lunch out of the slicker. Ordinarily Polkadot would have stopped the moment the reins dropped to the ground. But they hadn't dropped and they weren't likely to.

Pete jumped up, running, and yelling, "Whoah, Polkadot! Whoah!" If Polkadot heard, he paid no attention. Pete's slicker was hanging down on one side and slapping his legs at every step. The gentle Apaloosa was spooked and no doubt about it. Headed toward the canyon where camp lay, he ran as fast as he could in the rough country.

Furious with himself because of his careless following of a sudden impulse, Pete followed after him on foot. There was just a chance Polkadot might stop before he reached camp. If he didn't, Hatsy would be worried, and would come hunting for Pete. If Polkadot didn't return—Pete didn't want to think of this possibility.

Pete was so angry and humiliated that, when he saw a biscuit that had dropped out of the streaming slicker, he gave it a kick. Then he stopped short.

He was hungry, and it was just that kind of impulse that had got him into a jam. "I'm going to put me up one of those *think* signs," he said to himself.

About a mile from camp, Pete heard Hatsy calling in his thin, old voice, "Pete! Pete!"

Pete answered "Coming!" and gave a loud whistle.

"What in tarnation happened?" Hatsy said when they met.

Pete explained a little shamefacedly.

"You pull another stunt like that and you can spend the rest of the summer riding a burro at the ranch," Hatsy said. Without another word, he turned Polkadot back toward camp. Pete followed in silence.

Next morning Pete took Polkadot into the corral to be with Sandy. After the two horses had sniffed each other and Polkadot had walked around curiously, they quieted down and stood head to tail like old companions swatting flies off each other.

When they were thoroughly used to each other Pete went in with a rope, caught Polkadot, and led him round and round the corral. He did this several times, then led the horse outside. Then he roped Sandy and tried to lead him. At first Sandy balked, and stood braced, just shaking at the rope around his neck which was trying to make him do something he hadn't the impulse to do himself. Pete kept pulling steadily, but not enough to cut off the horse's wind. Then Sandy's patience gave way. He snapped his head back, nearly pulling Pete over onto his face.

"Snub," Hatsy called in a low voice and Pete ran

his rope around the tree trunk just in time to give Sandy a nasty jerk. He hadn't wanted to hurt Sandy at all while training him, but maybe this had to be done, to teach him respect for a rope and what it could do.

Sandy reared again and got a mean pull on his neck. Before he was thoroughly frightened Pete loosened the line, then pulled gently, then harder. The harder he pulled the more the rope hurt. When he slacked up, the rope cut less. When Sandy took a couple of steps toward Pete, the pressure of the rope around his neck eased off.

"Good horse, good Sandy. Come along, come along," Pete said approvingly as the horse took his first steps. He took more, and found the line always slack when he walked. Half an apple followed as a reward.

"Can I put on the hackamore now and try to lead him with that?" Pete asked Hatsy after a while.

"Why not? Who's stopping you?" Hatsy chirped back.

Sandy was as cautious about accepting the hackamore as he had been about being led by the lariat. But soon he was prancing around spiritedly, not trying to pull the lead rope from Pete's hand.

"Better let me in there with him a little now," Hatsy announced after Sandy had got thoroughly used to the hackamore. "The horse has got to get

"Good Horse, Good Sandy. Come Along."

used to both of us, and it will take both of us to finish him off."

At first Sandy was a little skittish about working with Hatsy, but he soon found the same gentleness, and the same rewarding sounds of friendship and approval.

It was now time for sacking out. Pete took a gunny sack from the wagon. "Watch out for his feet. This is when Sandy will show the buck in him, if he's going to be a bucker," Hatsy said.

Pete let Sandy get thoroughly used to the sight of the sack before he made a move. Sandy smelled it as it hung on the gate. He saw Pete carry it around in one hand. He got a lot of good looks at it as he stood with his hackamore tied to the snubbing post. Then Pete took the sack and touched Sandy with it gently on his back. Sandy shied and swung away from it. Pete touched him again—and again. And gradually he touched him all over his back. He did this a few minutes at a time, off and on, during the morning. Then he left the sack on Sandy's back.

A wriggle of Sandy's skin sent it sliding to the ground. "Don't worry. Don't get restless, Sandy, now we'll try it again," Pete said.

Patiently Pete replaced the sack as Sandy shook it off. Then he varied this training by getting Sandy used to hobbles. He and Hatsy, working together, with the horse tied to the snubbing post, quietly put soft leather hobbles on his forefeet for a few minutes. At each new restraint Sandy was restless, but he seemed to sense that none of his new experiences were bringing trouble.

He even accepted currying, which Pete did very gently at first using a brush only instead of a stiff currycomb.

At the end of the third week Sandy was used to more new things. Pete had roped him while riding Raindrop around the corral. Hatsy had roped him from Polkadot. They had both sacked him, and they had even got him used to a cinch holding the sack in place.

"Do you think he'll buck when we put the saddle on?" Pete asked.

"Lots of horses never buck," Hatsy said, "particularly horses that haven't been raised on a diet of spurs and quirts and bits that look like a combination hardware store and jewelry shop. Some horses show their spirit by fighting their riders. Others show it by learning. They have plenty of spirit— they just use it in the right way."

Before Pete actually tried to saddle Sandy he led him out of corral a few times and let him have his fill of good grass. Both Apaloosas were always along, and he was hobbled or tethered as he grazed, but he seemed to take this new freedom as part of all the new experiences he was enjoying.

Finally the time for saddling came. Pete let Sandy
smell the strange new thing and showed him the
saddle as it hung from the corral gate. Then he saddled Raindrop right close beside Sandy in the corral. At last, holding Sandy's hackamore and talking
soothingly to him as he stood hobbled by the gate,
Pete worked from the top bar on the gate and eased
the saddle over onto Sandy's back. He had tied the
stirrups over the saddle so there would be nothing
dangling between the horse's legs to frighten him.

Sandy shied as much as he could in his hobbles
and shook his head. But he calmed down quickly,
and Pete gave him a reassuring pat. He let Sandy
stand for a minute and then took the saddle off. Several more of these saddlings and unsaddlings followed. Then finally the saddle was cinched. Again
Sandy repeated his pattern of calming down after
the first unfamiliarity of a new experience had worn
off. Soon Pete removed the hobbles and let Sandy
free in the corral as he got used to the feel of the
saddle.

Before long Sandy accepted the saddle as if he'd
been born with one on his back. Then Pete tied a
sack with about fifty pounds of sand in it onto the
saddle. Sandy accepted the sack with no fuss at all.
The final test came next day. Hatsy hovered close,
bending his dry, small body to check the hobbles,
feeling the cinch to see that Sandy hadn't swelled up

when it was first tightened, as many a horse will do. Then he mounted Raindrop, dallied the lead rope around the saddlehorn, and pulled up the slack as he backed Raindrop away facing Sandy.

The big moment was here. Now came the test of whether Sandy had really accepted Pete. As he heaved up from the ground his weight pulled to the left on the saddle.

Sandy wriggled away from this surprisingly unbalanced load, and he moved so fast that Pete was thrown sideways onto the ground where he landed in the kind of roll he'd practiced hundreds of times on the football field. He was shaken up and surprised and very much humiliated.

Sandy looked around as Pete picked himself up and recovered his hat. His gentle Sandy had pitched him off before he'd even got in the saddle.

Hatsy for his part was one big grin. "Next time you better be ready to go where your horse goes," he cackled good-naturedly.

Pete turned his back.

He didn't want the old man to see his red face. He stood for a time stroking the excited horse, patting his neck and head, and talking to him in a voice so low he hoped Hatsy could not hear him.

"Sandy, I made another mistake. I tried two new things at once on you. You never had a man on your back. You never had a man climb into the saddle.

We'll start over again."

Pete led Sandy to the gate. Hatsy sat on Raindrop watching the performance. Then Pete climbed to the top bar, slid down into the saddle and sat there quietly. Sandy shook a little and looked around to see what this new-feeling thing was on his back.

In a minute, Hatsy started Raindrop walking slowly around the corral. Soon Sandy was following as if carrying a rider was the most natural thing in the world.

Pete was jubilant. He had done it. He was on his horse, and his horse had let him stay there.

CHAPTER ELEVEN

ASSORTED BAD HOMBRES

After Pete had ridden Sandy around the corral for a while and had got him used to being mounted from the ground, Hatsy, without saying a word, let down the gate bars. Then he swung up onto Raindrop and waited outside.

Filled with excitement and pride, Pete walked Sandy slowly out and down the stream toward the first campsite he and Hatsy had used. Before they quite reached it, he tried to turn Sandy back. He didn't want to ride him too close to his beloved dunes. The horse might take a notion to run and rejoin his band. But Sandy didn't turn in response to the pressure of the single line on the hackamore. It took a little worrying with the help of Hatsy and Raindrop close alongside to get him headed back for the corral. But finally he did turn back and covered the low flat ground at a quick trot before the canyon began to rise steeply into the heart of the great peak.

Then followed two days of practice with bit and bridle. There were hours of riding the horse inside the corral, and outside, too, in the little park, guiding him with the gentle pressure of reins on his neck.

Never once did Pete pull hard on the half-breed bit between the horse's jaws. Hatsy had told him this was the best bit for a cow pony. The spade, or U-shaped bend, in the bit was not high enough to give the horse great pain if the reins were pulled. "The cricket will give him something to play with," Hatsy said. He was talking about the little squeaky roller between the open ends of the spade which Sandy could turn with his tongue.

Many times Pete used his knees to press Sandy's sides and help indicate which way he wanted to turn. The horse began to find a way of pleasing his rider by turning the way the pressure of reins and legs indicated.

"Now at last," Pete said to himself, "I can ride Sandy anywhere. I caught him and gentled him all in a month."

"Let's do a little mountain climbing," Hatsy suggested one morning. "You've never been very far up this crick, and there's some pretty country to see."

Anything that combined riding and new country was fine with Pete. As they worked along the rough bottom of the creek beyond their little park, Pete enjoyed watching the muscles of his horse and feeling the power in them. There couldn't be a more sure-footed animal either, he kept thinking to himself while Sandy picked his way among boulders.

The whole world was brighter than it had ever

been. The pale blue columbine and the dark blue monkshood and flax were like splashes of the sky in the gravelly earth. Along the water were shooting stars with their yellow points and back-swept purple petals. Fringed blue gentians followed close to the creek, and higher on the hillside Indian paintbrush splashed red beneath the slender gray-green aspens.

At several points they rode into small parks like the one in which they were camped. In one of these they startled a fawn.

"Never saw a fawn as young as that one without a doe somewhere near," Hatsy said. "Maybe the doe is over the ridge, though, and will come back in a while."

"Come to think of it, there wasn't any doe with the fawn I got tangled up with the other day," Pete said. "Suppose this is the same one?"

"Not likely," Hatsy answered. "We're a long way from there, and too many things could happen to a little feller like that in a week. It's funny, though."

Sandy and Pete were in the lead as they turned a sharp bend. There the country became rougher. The horses had more difficulty picking their way. Just as Sandy worked cautiously around an outcropping boulder, he snorted, reared back, and spilled Pete off into the creek.

Sandy, riderless, lunged off downstream. But he stepped on the reins that dragged under his big feet.

The spade of the bit gave a sharp dig at the roof of his mouth, bringing him to a confused halt. Now Hatsy grabbed the reins and kept him from bolting.

Pete scrambled to his feet, drenched and confused. He shook the water out of his eyes and tried to see what had happened. The first thing that met his eyes was a small brown shape disappearing over a fallen log.

"Hey!" Pete yelled. "It looks like a bear cub." He turned looking for Sandy and saw his hat tumbling away down the creek.

"I got Sandy. You grab your hat," the old man called to him.

In another minute Pete had his sombrero and was at Sandy's side, stroking his neck and talking to him in a soothing voice. When the horse was calmed down, Pete looked up at Hatsy with some uncertainty. "What in the world did I do wrong that time?" he asked.

Hatsy grinned pleasantly and said, "There ain't a hoss that can't be rode, and there ain't a man that can't be throwed. In other words, it wasn't your fault. I never did know a horse that was friendly with bears. Raindrop would have spooked, too, if he'd been in the lead."

When Pete mounted Sandy again, the horse kept shying back from the place where he'd seen the bear. Finally Hatsy advised, "Let's not try to go on now.

We don't have to catch any trains. We better take Sandy back to camp and let him get the bear out of his system."

A heavy rain the next morning decided them not to ride at all. Instead they spent most of the day in the wagon where the canvas top kept them dry. Hatsy busied himself repairing moccasins while Pete wrote postcards to people at home.

Finally Hatsy broke a long spell of silence. "Being under canvas this way reminds me of the time I was in a tent at Creede, up north of here a ways. Creede was a rip-snorting mining camp in those days. The saying went that it was 'day all day in the daytime and there was no night in Creede.' I guess that was true for some of the gun-totin' bad men, but it didn't go for me. I was just a little shaver then—it was a couple of years before the Utes borrowed my scalp."

Hatsy paused a while as if to remember just how it was, then went on. "Well, I was asleep in our tent when gunfire in the next tent woke me up. I stayed kind of quiet until the shooting was over, and then I stuck my head out under the edge of the tent kind of inconspicuous like to see what the racket was about. It was about something all right. I saw a bunch of men my dad had told me were gamblers carrying Bob Ford out of the next tent, feet first and full of lead."

"You mean *the* Bob Ford?" Pete asked cautiously.

"Sure. There was only one Bob Ford as far as I knew. The name never got very popular those days among the kind of people that was looking for names for their prospective heirs. It was Bob Ford sure enough—the man who shot Jesse James. He'd made some prospector plenty mad about something. Most people seemed to feel that that prospector had cleaned up and beautified the scenery considerable by the trigger work he did, but mainly I was glad he hadn't made a mistake and poked his gun into the wrong tent. They were all just about alike, and crowded together a little too close for much target practice."

As Hatsy finished, Pete turned over on his back on his bedroll and stared at the gray canvas wagon cover above his head. He tried to imagine what it must have been like in the early days.

After a while he stretched, got up, and lifted the flap of the wagon. The unusual all-day rain showed no sign of stopping. Pete didn't particularly care, if he could get Hatsy to talk some more.

"Did you know anybody else like Bob Ford in the old days?" he asked.

"I can't say he was a personal friend of mine," Hatsy replied, "but I met up with Soapy Smith on that same trip to Creede. Seems Soapy ran the town. Every once in a while he would need a little extra cash, and he always got it quick and easy from folks like my dad and me. He saw us coming, and green- horn must have been written all over us. Anyway, he offered to sell us a bar of soap that was wrapped in a dollar bill, and he was only going to charge us a dollar for the whole thing. That seemed like a good bargain any way you looked at it. So Dad got a bar for himself and a bar for me, which wasn't exactly the kind of present I was hankering for just then. Funny thing was that when we got the soap those dollar bills had kind of evaporated. We never could figure out how Soapy lifted them. We thought we hadn't taken our eyes off them. But that experience taught me two things. One was how Soapy got his name and the other was that you never should trust paper money. I never carried anything but silver dollars since then."

"Is Creede still there?" Pete asked.

"Sure. But all the bad men and most of the good men, too, have cleared out," Hatsy answered. "Some of the tough hombres turned into cattle rustlers. There's always fellows like that around where there's a nickel to be made."

"There aren't rustlers any more, are there?" Pete said.

"Just as many as ever," Hatsy answered. "They got new-fangled ways of stealing cattle, though— same as ranchers got newfangled ways of growing them. Only last summer they caught Wall-Eyed Willie toting borrowed beef out of the valley in a fancy refrigerator truck. Next thing you know they'll be using helicopters."

"What do you mean, in a refrigerator truck?" Pete asked, not quite believing the story.

"Wall-Eyed Willie used to drive up at night, near where there was a likely bunch of critters. Then he and his men would slaughter a few, skin 'em, bury the hides, and heave the meat into the cooling truck. By next morning the meat would be in some butcher shop on the other side of the mountains."

"Hey!" Pete exclaimed. "Do you suppose Moore's a rustler?"

"Could be. But it doesn't seem too likely. His camp's up where the cattle don't run. Still we might look into it."

"Maybe those tire tracks we saw were a refrigerator truck," Pete insisted.

"And maybe they were nothing but Preacher Peeble's old pickup, too," Hatsy said. "He's the kind of minister who doesn't think a soul needs saving unless it lives a long way from any church. He's been known to go clear up above timberline to talk religion to some sheepherder."

"What about him?" Pete asked curiously.

"That's all about him," Hatsy answered. And Pete could see that even if it rained a week the old man was all caught up on talking.

So Pete pulled on his slicker and his moccasins, climbed down over the wheel of the wagon, and moved the tethered horses to fresh grazing places. As Pete came up, Sandy turned his wet head and nuzzled him. He didn't seem to mind the rain. After all, he'd spent his life outdoors in every kind of weather. Pete hoped it would clear the next day so he could get on with the horse's training.

CHAPTER TWELVE

SKI-JAW AND SALAMI

Next morning Pete thought it was still raining when he awoke in the wagon. There was a steady drip on the canvas. But he saw when he looked out that the sky was blue overhead, and the drip came from the soaked leaves of the trees all around.

"Come on, Hatsy. Let's saddle up," he said. "Rain's over."

"You tend to the horses while I get some of this wet wood to burning," Hatsy replied.

An hour later, with a good hot breakfast of flapjacks and fried eggs tucked away, Hatsy said, "Better saddle the Apaloosies today. The ground's too muddy for much riding, but we can teach Sandy how it feels to be led by someone on horseback."

Pete wanted only to ride Sandy, but he agreed that his mount should get used to everything a good horse ought to know. He wasn't surprised that Sandy acted a little skittish at first about following at Polkadot's heels or right beside him. But before long Sandy was acting as if he enjoyed traveling close to the other horses and Pete. "Someday," Pete thought to himself, "I'll teach him to follow without a rope." He knew it was too soon to try this now.

The hot sun quickly dried away signs of yesterday's rain, and by evening, Hatsy said they could take a trip out on the plains in the morning.

Before the direct rays of the sun reached them the following day Pete on Sandy and Hatsy on Raindrop were trotting along between clumps of greasewood and the sparse sagebrush growth at the western edge of the sand dunes. Pete touched his heels to Sandy's flanks, and loosened the reins in his left hand. He wanted to try the horse at a gallop.

Sandy at first did nothing but shake his head in a gesture of surprise and kept up his easy trot. Hatsy saw what was happening, and in a moment Raindrop streaked out ahead. Now Sandy broke into a gallop at once, and Pete gave him full freedom to race.

After a short sprint, Hatsy reined in his horse. But Sandy flew on with mane and tail streaming. Every rippling muscle seemed to show delight in this new physical freedom. He did not slow down when Pete pulled in lightly. Rather than give a painful tug on the reins, Pete touched Sandy lightly on the right shoulder with his toe and held the right rein against Sandy's neck. Responding perfectly, the horse swerved in a wide circle until they rejoined Raindrop who had slowed to a walk. Content now to walk beside the other horse, Sandy changed from a gallop to a trot and then fell into step.

Twice more Pete took short gallops and tried to rein in. But Sandy had not yet caught onto the meaning of Pete's light tug on the bit. He was bridle-wise, however. He had learned to turn as Pete pressed one rein or the other against his neck.

"That horse has a good trot and a good gallop," Hatsy said. "And he breaks from one to the other naturally. That's one thing you won't have to worry about. Later on we'll see what he can do about a canter."

Praise from Hatsy for the horse was all Pete needed. He had already been thrilled by the power and speed of the pony as they dashed over the level ground. Now he had a mount that could go places and do things. It wouldn't be long before he could ride Sandy proudly in to the ranch and go out with the hands when they looked after the cattle.

"How soon do you think I can show off Sandy at the ranch?" Pete asked.

"Seems like you never will get over being in too much of a hurry," Hatsy said. "There's a lot of things that pony doesn't know yet. Right now would be a good time to teach him something he's got to learn, too. He's got to find out what a saddlehorn's for. Think that one over."

Pete looked down at the horn in front of him and fingered it absent-mindedly for a minute.

Hatsy went on, "That thing's a working tool, in

"That Horse Has a Good Gallop," Said Hatsy

case you hadn't noticed. You can use it for a snubbing post when you're roping calves, and it comes in mighty handy when you want to drag a steer out of a swamp—or some firewood into camp. A cowpony has to learn what it feels like to have a lot of weight hitched to the saddlehorn."

"How do we start teaching Sandy that?" Pete asked.

"We can start with firewood first," Hatsy replied.

They turned back toward camp, and when they found a small fallen tree, Pete slipped the loop of his lariat around the big end of the trunk. Then he tied the rope to the saddlehorn and mounted again.

As the weight of the log dragged on the rope, Sandy shied and swung his hindquarters around. Pete had a job getting him to swing back into position where he could pull. But after several false starts, Sandy seemed to realize what was expected of him. He walked steadily on and the log jerked along behind over the uneven ground. "Good old Sandy," Pete said, and leaned down to pat his neck approvingly.

At times the pressure of the rope which ran across Pete's leg was uncomfortable. He realized suddenly how useful heavy bullhide cowboy chaps would be right now.

After they had got the log to camp, Pete dragged in two slightly heavier ones, while Hatsy stirred up a meal over the campfire.

"Want a little change from fishing this afternoon?" Hatsy said.

"Like what?" Pete asked.

"Like skiing. I seem to remember you told me you know how."

"I can ice skate, too. It would be a nice way to cool off. Let's go," Pete said.

Hatsy said nothing. He walked over to the wagon and rummaged around inside it for a minute. Then Pete saw a pair of skis slowly sliding out over the tailboard and dropping into the grass. A pair of ski poles followed, and after them sailed two ski boots.

"Got snow in there, too?" Pete called, laughing.

"Don't waste my time. Try those boots on," Hatsy said. "If they fit you, go saddle up Sandy and Raindrop."

Mystified, Pete tried on the boots. They felt strange and awkward after the pliable moccasins and the small, light cowboy boots he'd been wearing. But with extra socks on his feet, they fitted well enough.

"You got any canoes or rowboats in there, too?" Pete asked. The fact was, Hatsy did have a lot of stuff stowed in the wagon which Pete had never examined. After all, it was the old man's home the year round. "I thought you went south in the winter to get away from the cold. What do you need skis for?"

"They ain't mine," Hatsy confessed. "I borrowed 'em from Slim at the ranch. He claims he can ride 'em as well as he can a bronc, and he says they take him where a horse can't go when the snow's three feet deep. Nowadays they got gadgets for everything."

"Okay, so they're Slim's, but what are they doing here?" Pete asked.

"They're for you. You can go sand skiing on the dunes this afternoon, if you want to, and I sure want to watch."

Pete was amazed and very much excited. He'd never thought of the idea, but maybe it would work. "I'll try anything once, but the laugh will be on you and not me, if you have to dig me out of the sand."

With Hatsy carrying the ski poles and Pete riding with the skis over his shoulder, they went down to the nearest edge of the dunes. The early afternoon sunlight beat down intensely on the cream-colored mass and a warm wind carried wisps of dry sand off the ridges.

In snow, Pete would have herringboned up the steep slopes ahead, but he trudged up instead in the heavy ski boots, losing ground sometimes almost as fast as he gained. Underfoot the sand squeaked and scrunched. Every step made a kind of off-key music. Finally he was high enough so that he thought he could make a good try at sliding.

As he looked down, he felt the same kind of thrill

he always had at the top of a snow-covered slope before he made a swift swoop to the bottom. While he strapped on his skis, he thought how peculiar all this was. The hot summer sun beat down on his cowboy hat. He was sweaty from the climb. He tightened the chinstrap to hold the hat on, took a pole in each hand, and jumped into the air, turning so that his skis pointed straight downhill. "Powder River! Here I come!" he yelled at Hatsy.

To Pete's astonishment, he was skiing, and he was gathering speed. This was wonderful! With feet close together and knees acting as springs, he flew along. The run was brief, but he ended with a flourishing Christiania turn which sent out a great spray of sand from the sharply tilted edges of his skis, while the particles of sand beneath him raised a screech as he came to a stop.

"Mighty nice ride," Hatsy said. "You never pulled leather nor showed sky once. First time I ever saw two pieces of wood do anything like that."

Without taking his skis off, Pete turned and zigzagged up the slope. It was hard going, because the sand gave less support than most kinds of snow. This time he went much higher. Finally pausing on the crest of a ridge, he stopped to catch his breath. As he waited, he studied a series of ridges below. Instead of making a straight run, he would swing back and forth on the hill. The ride would be longer that

way, and he might get some little jumps as he sped
over the crest of each ridge.

Waving a pole at Hatsy, he shoved off with a long,
strong gliding stride. His knees quickly got the feel
of the shifting contour of the sand, and he banked
from the side of one ridge down into a hollow, then
up over the crest of the next. He had enough speed,
and with a little leap he was in the air, skis and all.
Leaning well forward, he held his balance as the
wood slapped down on the sand. Now he was off
again and in great skidding turns swept first to his
right, then to his left all the rest of the way down,
leaving a graceful, snaky trail behind him.

At the bottom he came to a dead stop—not by
turning this time but by snowplowing and ending
with a quick jump at right angles to the slope of the
hill.

"Hey, Hatsy! That was a wonderful idea you had.
Want to try it?"

"There's a lot of things could happen on that hill
besides what you're doing, and they'd happen to
me," Hatsy replied. "When I can't drive a wagon or
ride a horse, I'll walk. But I sure like watching you.
You even make it look easy."

"One thing isn't easy, and that's climbing up,"
Pete said. "Snow's a lot better for that, and it's not
so hot."

"Too bad you can't ride your horse up," Hatsy

said. "He's used to traveling in those dunes."

Pete suddenly had an idea. "Hatsy, would you be willing to ride Sandy?"

Hatsy hesitated, then said, "Sure, but what for?"

"Would you ride him up on the dunes?" Pete urged.

"Sure, but what good would that do?"

"Sandy's learned how to drag wood," Pete explained. "Let's see if he'll drag me up the hill."

Hatsy grinned. "Now that's what I call real good horse sense," he chuckled.

Pete wondered whether Sandy would accept Hatsy, and he could see that the old man wondered, too. After he mounted, with no protest from Sandy, he rode around for a few minutes, turning this way and that. Pete knew he wanted to get the feel of the horse and get the horse used to him, too.

Then Hatsy turned Sandy around toward Pete and gave him one end of the lariat. The other he fastened to the saddlehorn.

"I'll carry your poles up," Hatsy said.

"And I'll stay well behind," said Pete. "I'll steer to one side so you won't be bothered by the rope on your leg. Now, let's see what happens. You better not try to switch back and forth, the way I did going up. Just keep angling on up in one direction. We can swing back later to where I can slide."

Sandy looked around with interest at his burden

as Hatsy touched him with his heels. Then he stepped out with his big feet and headed on a gentle incline up the rising dune.

"This is the life!" Pete said to himself. His own horse acting as a ski tow. He wanted to let out a holler of pleasure to Hatsy, but he knew he might frighten Sandy. He just held onto the rope, which he had passed around his body without fastening a loop or a knot, so that he could grasp both strands in his two hands in front of him. He hadn't made a knot, because he wanted to be able to let go when he needed to.

Although being towed this way was easier than climbing, the steady tension in his leg muscles be-

gan to tell. Soon the tops of his thighs had a hot, burning sensation. Pete wanted a rest. "Hatsy," he called quietly. "Hold up for a minute. I'm tired."

Hatsy stopped and turned in the saddle. *"You're* tired! I thought it was the horse that was doing the work."

Pete explained that his legs were actually doing a lot of work, even though he wasn't moving them.

"Well, I vum," Hatsy said. "You're never too old to learn." He and Sandy waited patiently till Pete was ready to go on.

After his next rest, Pete decided to try an experiment. "Hatsy, we're going to skijore now," he said.

"How's that?"

"You get Sandy to go as fast as he can, not uphill, but on a level course right along the side of the dunes, here," Pete said. "Let him really go. When I get tired, I'll just let loose of the rope."

"What did you say that's called?" Hatsy asked.

"Skijoring," Pete said. "I've never tried it, but I've seen pictures of it being done in the snow."

"Let's go," said Hatsy, and he urged Sandy ahead, first at a walk, then at a fast trot.

Pete leaned back against the rope, and his hands ached with the strain. But the pleasure of skimming over the sand was enough to make him keep on until he could hold no longer. Behind the speeding pony, he glided first in a straight course, then swinging in gentle arcs from left to right. Finally, panting, he dropped the rope and turned uphill to a slow stop.

When Hatsy returned with his ski poles, Pete said, "Boy, was that fun! Thanks a lot." He patted the horse. "Good boy, Sandy. I hope we can do this when there's real snow sometime."

Pete was beginning to feel rested now. "I'm going to angle back toward a good high place," he said. "Then I'll take a long run back down and meet you where we started. It will unlimber my legs to go up by myself instead of being towed. This time I'm going to slalom down the hill." He looked out of the corner of his eye at Hatsy.

"First it's ski-jawing, then it's salami," the old

man snorted.

"Anyway, it's no boloney." And Pete took off up the slope.

At the top of a rise, he flopped down in the sand to rest and wait till Hatsy and Sandy had rejoined the Apaloosa on the ground below. Finally, he saw the old man dismount and give the horse a friendly slap. He almost hated to start this last slide down. It was sheer delight to lie relaxed in the hot sand high on the dunes looking down at his horse, then up at the great mountains towering above. He didn't know when he'd ever have such a day again.

But at last, tucking his knees up close under him and heaving with his poles, he rose up and with a long running glide started down the slope. Faster and faster he went, till the hot air lashing at his eyes brought tears. Now he began to switch back and forth from right to left in quick, skidding turns. At each turn the sand squealed and sprayed out. Pete was pretending this was a slalom course and imagined the flags set at different points where he made the turns to get around them. Each imaginary flag slowed him down a little, but between them he gained speed. As he approached the bottom, he cut loose with one long straight run that ended in a daring jump turn. Leaning forward with both ski poles to his left, he thrust them into the sand, then swung his skis high into the air and slapped them

down at right angles to his course. All this brought
him to a sudden, jolting stop, exactly in front of
Hatsy.

"Them ain't my skis," the old man remarked.
"Slim didn't lend them to me for kindling. You better watch out."

But Pete knew that Hatsy wasn't worried. He
could tell, too, that the old man had been pleased by
the skill he had shown. He was breathless and dripping with sweat. He unbuckled the ski binding and
hobbled off the sand to the nearest aspen. There he
stretched out in the shade and slowly got his breath.

"That was some workout," he said when Hatsy
approached.

"I can't see what there is about sliding downhill
that gets you in such a lather."

"I was using every muscle in my body," Pete replied. When he recovered he said, "I hope you got a
lot of chuck lined up for tonight. I'm going to be
plenty hungry. But before that I'm going to surprise
the trout by taking a good cold bath in the creek."

CHAPTER THIRTEEN

DUCK-POND RAIDER

Pete groaned and pulled himself out of the bedroll. Every muscle in his legs ached, and his shoulders and arms were sore, too. He had thought he was in good condition—he'd done a lot of riding and hiking in the last few weeks. But skiing had found muscles he'd obviously not been using.

Hatsy watched him as he limped around and finally said, "I kinda got a notion that a day in the saddle would take some of that salami out of you. Let's saddle up and ride out on the flats. It will do Sandy good, too."

The creek still roared and tumbled from the spell of rain they'd had. The flowers were brighter and the leaves crisp and shiny. As Pete jogged slowly down toward the plains, he realized the rain probably had made more changes than he'd noticed before.

Sandy obviously felt a good deal fresher than Pete did. When he reached the great open valley, he exploded into a gallop. Pete's aching muscles made him stiff and awkward in the saddle at first. But before long he had warmed up and relaxed.

As Sandy flew on, Pete saw a prairie-dog town ahead—reined in, alarmed. Hundreds, maybe thousands, of little mounds dotted the earth. On each mound, sitting bolt upright, was a fat, reddish-brown prairie dog. Gradually Pete pulled Sandy to a halt. He didn't want the horse to race through the prairie-dog town and step into one of the animal's burrows by mistake. He knew that was an almost certain way for a horse to break a leg.

Pete decided to wait there while Hatsy caught up. Now he could hear the puppy-like bark of prairie dogs who had seen him and were giving the alarm. As Hatsy rode up, Pete pointed to the town, and they walked the horses slowly toward it. The scolding barks suddenly ended, and the entire community of prairie dogs dove underground, almost at the same time.

"I wouldn't let that pony get the idea you're training him for the Kentucky Derby, Pete," he said seriously. "Cow horses don't have much call to be racing around the range like that—except, of course, in a movie."

"I know, but figure how Sandy feels," Pete came back at him. "He's just naturally got a lot of energy in his system. He ought to work it out once in a while, oughtn't he?"

"No harm done. You know me, Pete. I generally want to speak about something, and this time it's that. You showed good sense when you stopped, though. Those dog holes are sure murder for horses."

Hatsy paused, then went on. "Nothing friendlier than a prairie dog ever came off the Ark, though. I used to have one for a pet, when I was a kid. He lived in his own hole out behind our cabin, but come mealtime he was always right there in the house, begging for sugar and bread."

"No fooling!" Pete said.

"I'm telling you the honest truth," Hatsy said. "He used to follow me around like a puppy. But come night he'd vamoose."

Pete saw Hatsy wasn't joking. He halfway wished he had a tame prairie dog, too. But right now he had Sandy and that was plenty to ask for.

They were past the prairie-dog town now, and they let the horses out into a good, easy traveling pace. For a long time they rode in silence. The landscape ahead began to change.

"Better take it easy from now on," Hatsy warned as they approached a great stretch of swampy land. Off to the right Pete could see a glimmer of open water.

"Finest duck-hunting place in the world," Hatsy commented. "Thousands of ducks stop here every spring and fall going north or south. Plenty of 'em live here all summer long, too, but of course it's not hunting season till after frost sets in. Some just hang around all the time where the underground cricks bubble up and the water never freezes."

They kept their horses on dry solid ground, circling around the marshy area. From time to time they caught glimpses of open patches of water. On several of these they saw little groups of ducklings swimming.

"Never saw ducklings this size without a mother duck bossing them around," Hatsy observed.

Later they did see many ducks out on the deeper water. But there still continued to be groups of ducklings alone near the shore, without the busy presence of a mother.

A sudden picture of the two lone fawns crossed Pete's mind. Could there be any connection between fawns without does and ducklings without ducks? But before he had a chance to try the idea out on Hatsy, the old man dismounted and to Pete's amazement took off his Levis.

Then, without a word, he waded barelegged in his moccasins out into the swamp. He pushed cattails aside, peering everywhere. Finally he called back, "I got it. Come and have a look."

Pete jumped down, tied Sandy to a low-growing shrub, shed his clothes, and waded out. There, hidden from dry land, was a duck, hanging from a string attached to a long limber branch that had been thrust deep in the mud.

"Somebody's poaching and catching these ducks with fishing hooks," Hatsy said with authority and anger in his voice. "Meanest way to kill a bird, and I'd like to find out who the coyote is who's doing it. It's easy to see now why so many ducklings and so few ducks."

A little farther along they found another line, this time with a duckling caught on it. The sight of the duckling infuriated Hatsy. "Poaching is bad enough," he fumed. "But a little one this size, too small to eat, is just mean and wasteful."

They circled on around the marsh and discovered half a dozen more lines but with no ducks on them. These they pulled out of the water. "Let's just roll up the lines and put them in my saddlebag," Hatsy said. "I'm going to report this to the game warden. I'll take 'em back to the ranch for evidence along with the ducks we found."

As they went on around the marsh, they saw tracks of big rubber boots near two more baited fishing lines.

"Who do you suppose is doing this?" Pete asked.

"It's not somebody who's hungry and trying to get a duck for supper," Hatsy replied. "Maybe a tourist who thinks it's smart to go home with a carload of game."

"The guy who set these traps ought to be coming back sometime soon to unload them," Pete said. "Let's wait around and catch him in the act."

"You saw too many movies back in Chicago,"

Hatsy snapped. "Just take a look around here. Anybody can see our horses for miles. No poacher's going to collect ducks while we're decorating the scenery. Besides that, he might have some unpleasant hardware along with him."

"Who's been seeing movies now?" Pete said with a grin.

"Tourists see 'em, too," Hatsy retorted. "But this fellow might be a poacher who's real serious about getting ducks and doesn't want to be bothered. I'm going to let the game warden handle this one."

They worked their way back to the place where they had left the horses.

"Do you want to ride in with me to the ranch?" Hatsy asked. "There's still time today, and I'd like to get word to the game warden."

"No, I'd rather not show Sandy off just yet," Pete replied. "I'll stay and get him used to having me swing a rope while I'm in the saddle."

"I may not get back till tomorrow night," Hatsy said as he started Raindrop off at a fast walk toward the ranch.

"Maybe I'll have a mess of fish for you," Pete said.

Trotting along north, Pete sat easily in the saddle. He was beginning to get the feel of Sandy and he liked the horse's quick, easy motions. After a while he took his rope from beside the horn of the saddle, opened up a good loop, and made a couple of swings

over his head. Sandy jumped sideways almost like a
cat at the unexpected movement in the air above his
eyes. But Pete kept his balance with more assurance
than he had when Sandy shied at the bear. His legs
seemed to telegraph to him just what motions Sandy
was going to make. Leaning over the horn, he patted
the horse's neck and talked soothingly to him.

He rode on a little and made more swings with
his rope. Gradually Sandy accepted the new experience. Every few hundred yards, Pete varied the routine by giving a light equal pull on both reins. He
wanted Sandy to learn to stop quickly after a cast
with the rope. Later he'd teach him to brace himself
against the tug of a calf caught in the loop of the
lariat. In a very short time the horse had learned the
signal to stand in his tracks.

As Pete approached the north end of the dunes, he
made a quick cast at a greasewood bush and caught
it. With a swift twist of the lariat around the horn,
he knotted it, and there was a sudden sidewise tug
on the saddle, which surprised Sandy. Pete's pull on
the reins, however, stopped him, and Sandy merely
looked around as if to see what this new pressure on
the saddle meant. Sandy could have pulled the bush
up by its roots, but Pete wanted him to learn to obey
each command. He dismounted, loosened the loop,
and recoiled his rope.

Pete couldn't help wishing Hatsy'd been there to

see what a good performance he and Sandy were putting on. He was sure now that Sandy would be ready
for roping calves at branding time next year. Maybe
not the biggest ones, but at least he'd be useful.

No horse from the ranch, not even Crackerjack
would have given him the fun he was having with
Sandy. Pete was about to break into a triumphant
gallop when he saw a cow with a little late calf beside
her ambling along a couple of hundred yards toward
the left. Why not rope the calf, just for practice?
Pete galloped ahead with a purpose.

The cow and calf fled, and Sandy seemed to join
in the spirit of the chase. The calf was no match for
his fast hoofs, and Pete managed to get in close to the
scared little animal's left side. Before it could dodge
like a jack rabbit, as calves often do, Pete had
dropped his loop over its neck and signaled for
Sandy to stop. But there was too much of the chase
in Sandy to come to a quick halt. The calf shot across
in front of him with the rope pulling across Sandy's
big chest. It almost tripped him up, and he was confused and excited.

Now Pete was frightened. Sandy could fall and
break his neck. The calf might be killed, too. Almost
in panic, he reined back hard. The painful dig of the
spade on the roof of the horse's mouth brought him
to a sudden stop. Pete nearly flew over the horn. The
calf struggled, but Sandy stood. Bawling and shak-

Pete Dropped a Loop on the Calf

ing her head ominously, the old cow trotted back
now. Pete knew he had to let the calf go, but he
wasn't sure how to do it. He was afraid Sandy might
spook if he dismounted, and he didn't want to get
in the way of the furious cow. He knew what he
was supposed to do. He ought to jump down and
walk toward the calf, holding the rope taut. He'd
have to take the chance.

With a reassuring pat on Sandy's neck, he dismounted and walked down the rope to the calf.
Keeping a wary eye out for the cow, Pete held the
rope tight and thus forced the jerking head of the
calf toward him.

Then he reached out gingerly, loosened the
honda, and flipped the rope off. With a deep gasp
for breath, the calf turned and ran bawling to its
mother.

Pete scrambled back on Sandy who was excited
but had stepped on the reins and had been stopped
by the pain of the bit.

As Pete quieted Sandy, he became aware of the
sound of pounding hoofs. Looking up, he saw a cowboy racing toward him. He was pretty sure it must
be one of Uncle Lem's hands, although he couldn't
tell positively. He didn't want anybody from the
ranch to see him on Sandy yet.

Without waiting to finish coiling his rope, he
touched Sandy's flanks with his heels and headed for

the dunes at a gallop. Sandy heaved up on the first
ridge in the dunes. Looking back, Pete saw that the
cowboy had stopped where the sand began. Sandy
could go where none of the ranch horses could. Cutting across the dunes, he left the baffled cowboy far
behind.

On top of a high ridge, he turned and got another
glimpse of the cowboy out on the flats. A broad grin
spread over Pete's tanned face. "I sure fooled that
fellow," he thought and he relished every bit of
pleasure and excitement in his escapade.

Then suddenly he began to have a small doubt.
He really had no business roping a calf right now.
What if he'd injured the animal? This time he'd
been lucky, but he remembered some of the times
he hadn't been. Not nearly so satisfied with himself
as he had been a few minutes before, he turned
Sandy east across the end of the dunes toward camp.

CHAPTER FOURTEEN

SANDY DISAPPEARS

Pete wasn't happy about his catch the next morning, either. He'd only been able to get four trout in a long morning's casting—and they were not big ones either. Hatsy, he suspected, would have brought back eight or ten. Still, the old man had been fishing about sixty years longer than Pete had. "Anyway, there's enough for supper," he decided, as he wrapped the trout in long, damp grass and put them in the covered bucket which he weighted down with a stone in the water at the edge of the creek.

He crossed the creek now and headed toward the corral. "Sa-a-a-ndy!" he called. "Sa-a-andy!" He planned to saddle his horse and ride to meet Hatsy.

But at the corral gate he stopped short. The bars were down and Sandy was not there. He called again, louder this time. By now Sandy knew his name, and Pete thought he would come in response to the call. Then suddenly he stopped. Why in the world were the bars down? No horse could have pulled them out. Hatsy wouldn't have gone off with Sandy without letting him know. Somebody had stolen Sandy!

Pete ran upstream a few hundred feet to the spot where he had tethered Polkadot. The Apaloosa was

168

grazing peacefully. Almost without thinking, Pete snatched up the rope and led Polkadot back to the wagon. Now he wondered if anything else had been stolen. A quick glance seemed to indicate nothing was gone. The saddle was in the wagon. The chuck box hadn't been disturbed. Only one thing had happened—Sandy had disappeared.

Quickly Pete threw the Navaho saddle blanket on Polkadot's back and saddled him. He'd have to look for Sandy. One idea kept bobbing up in his mind. He remembered the afternoon he had fallen asleep when Moore had been spying on Sandy in the corral. Maybe Moore had some interest in the horse. If Sandy was loose, he would probably head for the dunes. But if he had been stolen, the first place to look was Moore's camp.

Pete urged Polkadot up the side of the mountain as fast as he dared. The nimble Apaloosa heaved higher and higher on the direct line to Moore's camp. Suddenly Pete realized he'd forgotten to do something he knew Hatsy would have done. He hadn't looked for footprints around camp or any kind of trail showing where Sandy might have gone. For a moment he hesitated. Perhaps he should go back. But he decided he'd already come so far he might as well push on.

In spite of an urgent feeling that he must hurry, Pete reined in and gave the panting horse a rest. The trees opened out here and he could see some of the mountainside between him and the dunes. Suddenly Polkadot pricked up his ears and was all attention. Pete strained to pick up whatever sound the horse had heard.

From ahead and above, came the sound of something crashing in the brush, then the unmistakable beat of hoofs. Could it be Sandy? The sound was coming closer. For a moment Pete was undecided whether to head forward and investigate or wait. But waiting wasn't in him. He had to find out if it was Sandy.

Pete urged Polkadot straight ahead to intercept the crashing animal, which seemed to be going toward the dunes. And then it happened. He rode into a little clearing, and there speeding across in front of him, not a hundred yards away, was Sandy now at a full gallop. And he was dragging a rope behind him. That rope will catch something and break Sandy's neck, was Pete's first thought. He touched his heels to Polkadot, who leaped across the clearing after the fleeing horse. At the sound of pursuit, Sandy gave one frightened glance back, then dodged among the aspens.

With a terrible surge of fear, Pete saw Sandy snapped off his feet and thrown to the ground. The dangling rope *had* caught around a tree and jerked him down. But the next instant Sandy was scrambling back to his feet, apparently unharmed. Seeing the charging horse and rider now very close upon him, Sandy dodged back out of the woods and into the clearing.

Pete had had no time to think how he would catch Sandy, but now he made a lightning decision. He'd try his lariat. Quickly building a loop, he spurred Polkadot on. The Apaloosa seemed to know exactly what to do. He cut ahead of the fleeing mustang and brought Pete close enough to make a cast.

Pete let the loop sail out through the air. Polkadot automatically skidded to a stop and braced himself. Almost too late, Pete flipped the rope around the saddlehorn, then felt the terrific jerk. He'd made a good throw. Again Sandy was down.

Skilled cowpony that he was, Polkadot kept the rope taut, as Pete tied it firmly to the saddlehorn.

Just as he had done the day before, when he lassoed the calf, Pete walked the rope, hand over hand, toward Sandy who had scrambled to his feet and was beginning to run in a wide arc around Polkadot. As Sandy ran, Polkadot swung so that he always faced the frightened horse. Pete approached Sandy slowly, talking as he had always talked at the corral. Little by little Sandy calmed down and Pete was able at last to stroke his neck. Finally the horse stood quivering and seemed slowly to regain the feeling that he was once more among friends.

Pete stood by him a long time, stroking his damp sides and talking to him—and thinking. Sandy had not been let loose. He had been led out of the corral and the lead rope was one he had never seen. Sandy had also been running away from the place where Pete knew Moore's camp lay. It all added up in Pete's mind to a conviction that Moore had tried to steal Sandy. And the surer he was, the madder he got.

Pete was just about to take his lariat off Sandy's neck when Sandy lifted his head and ears and looked intently toward the upper edge of the clearing. A second later, Moore appeared on Bridger.

Sandy swung away with such force that Pete was almost pulled over flat on his face. Then Sandy be-

gan swinging in a wide arc again at the end of the
rope. But Polkadot stood his ground, swinging always with his head toward Sandy and backing up a
few steps once in a while to keep the rope taut. Pete,
holding to both the lariat and the lead rope was being pulled along after Sandy.

"Get out of here!" he shouted angrily across the
clearing. "I can't do anything with this horse while
you're around."

But Moore sat there on Bridger, watching the performance with a grin on his face.

"Get out!" Pete yelled again. "Can't you see
you're spooking my horse?"

"Who says he's your horse?" Moore called back.

"I don't see any brand on him, and I know where
you got him."

The loud voices made Sandy harder to control
than ever. In desperation Pete cried, "Beat it, you
horse thief!"

"Go ahead and have your fun," Moore called,
turning Bridger. "What makes you think anybody
would want a mean animal like that anyway?" And
he disappeared into the trees.

At last Pete got Sandy under control again. When
both horses were thoroughly rested, he mounted
Polkadot and walked him slowly down the mountain to camp, leading Sandy behind. It was a good
thing, he thought to himself, that he had trained
Sandy to be led this way. But on the other hand, no
one could have taken him out of the corral in the
first place, if he hadn't been trained. Anyway, Sandy
was back, and Pete was determined that nothing like
this would happen again.

It was late afternoon when Pete wearily turned
down the last slope into camp and saw Hatsy approaching from the downstream side.

The old man looked sharply at the exhausted
horses. "What're you up to, pardner? Looks like you
been trying to run that mustang of yours to death."

Pete said nothing until he had put Sandy in the
corral and shoved the bars back into place. Then, as
he unsaddled the two Apaloosas, he told Hatsy the

story of what had happened.

"That coyote Moore seems to be pretty desperate for a pack animal," Hatsy said when Pete had finished. "Back at the spread there, Lem told me Moore had been trying to buy the other burro. Said the first one up and kicked the bucket. But Lem wouldn't sell. Could be Moore figured Sandy'd make a pack horse. He's a smart devil if he is so sure nobody would get the law on him for stealing an unbranded mustang off a greenhorn from Chicago."

What Hatsy said made Pete feel better. "I'm hungry," he said. "What did Aunt Clara send?"

"This," Hatsy said, opening his saddle bag. He pulled out a head of iceberg lettuce. "Looks like Clary thinks you're a rabbit." Pete grinned, pulled the head open, and began to munch. Hatsy reached into the bag again. "And this." He pulled out a big crochet hook. "She says this is for you to use now that I told her you finished weaving those rag rugs. She wants you to put a lace edge on 'em."

Pete guffawed, and Hatsy pulled out quickly a whole roasted chicken, a loaf of Aunt Clara's home- made bread, and a jar of her wild raspberry jam. They sat down and went to work on the chicken, Pete using the crochet hook for a fork, with his little finger extended straight out, as fancy as he could hold it. Hatsy untied the dusty handkerchief from around his neck, spread it out with much ado in his lap, and used it delicately as a napkin. When he had finished his chicken, he reached over where his lariat lay, deftly swung a loop overhead, and lassoed the coffeepot from a rock by the dead campfire. The pot clattered as he pulled it toward him, and he said with great elegance, "Waiter, a demmy tassy, *if* you please."

Pete laughed and built a fire while Hatsy told him what had been happening at the ranch. Slim had given up trying to break Crackerjack, and Uncle Lem had sold the horse to a man who bought broncs for rodeos.

"How did you and the game warden come out?" Pete asked.

"Danged old fool let his connecting rod break and run straight through the block. Always did tell him he'd be better off on horseback, than in one of those stink wagons. Besides, he had a pig farrowing and he's sitting by his telephone expecting to win a million dollars on some radio prize program. So he gave me the job of un-poaching this neck of the woods. Meet the new deputy game warden, son."

"Does that mean no poached eggs for breakfast?" Pete asked. And then he added seriously, "What are we going to do about whoever is getting ducks over there at the lake? Do you think it's Moore, maybe?"

"I doubt it. He's up to something he needs a pack animal for, and Bridger could have carried all the ducks we found. But one thing we can do is to make ourselves kind of numerous all around these parts so as to scare off anybody who's hunting out of season," Hatsy said. Then he paused, obviously getting ready to spring something he had saved for the right moment. "Lem tells me there's a rustler we ought to look out for, too. Appears some fellow riding a mustang has been trying to make off with one of the Lazy B-5 calves. In fact, Pedro would have caught him except he vamoosed right into the dunes."

Pete snorted. "Well, anyway I found out I could rope a calf," he said. "Do they think I'm a rustler, sure enough?"

"They don't know it's you, but they're sure there's a rustler, and Lem was fixing to follow you with a posse until I told him you and I could take care of the situation. Being a deputy game warden, I've sort of got the law behind me."

As Pete led Sandy down to the creek for water a little later, he got to thinking about Moore again. Why was he so anxious to get a pack animal? Hatsy's talk of rustlers made him wonder whether the man was fixing to butcher calves and carry them where they could be taken out by the car or truck whose tracks they had seen.

When he returned to the campfire, he mentioned the idea to Hatsy. The old man said he'd been thinking the same thing. "But thinking's not going to solve any problems," he added. "We just have to keep our eyes peeled. Now I'm going to hit the hay."

Whether Moore was a rustler or not, Pete couldn't help hoping that he and Sandy would find some way of getting even with him.

CHAPTER FIFTEEN

MURDERED MUSTANGS

Next morning Hatsy grumbled and complained while he and Pete fixed breakfast. "I knew no-good would come of going back to the ranch without my soogans," he said. "Had to sleep in a bed and it near broke my back. Couldn't tell from one minute to the next what part of that infernal thing would give way under one part of me or another. It was like trying to get comfortable on top of a cloud—and about as safe. My back still feels like it's broke in about a dozen places."

He winced as he leaned over to take hold of the long handle of the frying pan, and when he sent the flapjack in the pan sailing into the air, it landed half on the side of the pan instead of all in the middle.

"I'm sorry your back hurts," Pete said. "Is there anything I can do to help?"

"The best thing you can do is to go out on Sandy and while you're riding think up some way to get rid of all the beds in the world."

Pete laughed and began to saddle up. He knew the old man wouldn't let him do anything to help, even if he did stay around camp.

As he rode down toward the dunes, he decided to

spend the day trying to find out something about the
auto tracks that he had seen leading into Moore's
camp. He already knew they came from the south,
so he planned to circle around the edge of the dunes
and visit the camp from that direction.

Sandy's pace was a sheer delight to Pete as he
broke into an easy lope where the ground above the
dunes opened out. He enjoyed the strong rhythm of
the horse, the morning air, which was still cool, and
the intense sunlight which filled the valley and was
reaching into the trees and canyons away above him
to the left.

Reining Sandy down to a walk he turned out onto
the edge of the dunes at the point where they lay
highest against the mountain. Soon now he would
turn back up toward Moore's place.

Then he saw marks above the dunes—two parallel
lines in the grass and gravel—tire tracks. They
pointed toward the dunes, but if there ever had been
tire tracks on the sand itself, wind had covered them
up.

Pete turned his horse out into the dunes. Maybe if
he rode out a little way he could find something that
would help explain those tracks.

Sandy, however, became nervous after he'd gone
only a short way. He danced and reared a little and
sidestepped, but he refused to go forward. Pete was
kept so busy managing the horse that he couldn't get

a good look ahead to see what might be frightening him.

"I wonder if you're remembering things about these dunes—and figuring how nice it would be to have a run here without me on your back," Pete said to Sandy. But Pete soon decided there was more than this behind the horse's behavior. He was jittery, uncertain. Then suddenly he snorted and whirled round, streaking it for the mountainside. Pete tried to control him only when they reached solid ground. There, after he had quieted the terrified animal, he tied him in an aspen grove and returned to the dunes on foot.

Behind a small ridge of sand, he found what had frightened Sandy—the body of a recently killed mustang. The coyotes hadn't discovered it yet, and Pete could see a small bloody hole in the mustang's chest.

"Somebody shot this mare," Pete said to himself. "That's a mighty mean thing to do."

He walked back off the dunes.

Before he mounted again, he wanted to have a look at the tire tracks. The treads that had made them were large, and as Pete stepped from one track to the other, he had a feeling there was something special about them, but at first he wasn't sure what it was. Then he remembered something. Back in Chicago, when snow lay on the streets, ordinary automobile tracks were exactly two of his strides apart.

But when he stepped across these tracks, his stride seemed to be longer—or else the tracks were closer together. And he was sure he hadn't grown that much since last winter. Clearly this couldn't be the trail of a truck or an ordinary car. It must have been made by a jeep. In fact, a jeep was about the only thing that could get around in this roadless mountain country. And, of course, Moore had appeared at the ranch that first time in a jeep.

It seemed to Pete that the tracks merely led from the direction of Moore's camp to the edge of the dunes and back again. He couldn't see what the man would be doing that for—after all, he had a horse for short trips, and the distance from here to the camp wasn't long. He felt sure, too, that Moore must be connected somehow with the dead mustang. But how? Why had he killed it?

Clearly Moore must have still another road into his camp from the south. The dunes were not a good roadbed for even a jeep with four-wheel drive and heavy treads. With this in mind, Pete decided to push on farther to the south and see what he could discover.

Sandy was calmed down now, and Pete rode along close to the edge of the sand. He hadn't gone far when Sandy spooked again. A little way to the right Pete caught a glimpse of something sticking up through the sand. He tried to ride toward it, but the horse refused. He wheeled and fought against the pressure of the reins. Pete did not want to bully Sandy into anything. So he let him follow his own head off into another grove of aspens where Pete tied him again.

Plodding out into the dunes on foot, Pete found that some freak wind had exposed a skeleton. He was sure it had a horse's skull—probably it had been another mustang. Obviously it wasn't an old skeleton, weathered and white. There were still bits of decayed flesh clinging to the bones which had been strewn around by coyotes. It certainly looked as if someone was after the mustangs. If it was Moore, why on earth did he want to kill the horses and simply leave them?

On his way back to Sandy, Pete decided he would not push on farther south. Instead he would ride up, visit Moore's camp again, and see what he could find out there.

In half an hour he reached the edge of the glade where Moore had set up the tents. Keeping upwind of the camp, he rode along just out of sight of it, so that Sandy wouldn't spook again. Behind a low ridge, he hobbled his horse and walked the rest of the way. Between the tents, he saw Moore with his back turned, adjusting the saddle on Bridger.

"Hello," Pete called.

Moore jumped and swung around facing Pete.

"What do you want?" he asked in an angry, startled voice.

On the spur of the moment, Pete said, "Oh, Hatsy and I ran out of sugar and thought maybe we could borrow a little."

"You can get it at your ranch," Moore answered sourly. "And when you're there, why don't you stay there? For your information, I'm only interested in company that I invite."

"I didn't mean to butt in," Pete said, trying to appear friendly. "But I didn't see any harm in asking." Pete glanced around the camp, and off to one side he saw something that hadn't been there before. Leaning against a tree was an archer's target, and near the sleeping tent was a large bow with some arrows. Now he remembered that when Moore came to the ranch that first day, Hatsy had seen a bow and arrows in the jeep.

Moore noticed Pete's interested glance at the archery equipment, and his attitude changed. "The doc who sent me up here said I needed some light exercise. I've been practicing with that setup."

"Let's see you shoot," Pete said.

Moore picked up the bow, shouldered the quiver full of arrows, and walked off a long way from the target. With what seemed to Pete like incredible speed, the man shot arrow after arrow into the target. In no time, ten of them were bunched in and

"You're Good," Pete Told Moore

around the bull's-eye.

"You're good," Pete said. "Are you as good with a gun?"

Moore looked at him sharply. "I don't have a gun. Wouldn't have one around. I saw all I wanted of them in the war," Moore snapped. "Now don't you think it's about time you beat it out of here?"

"I'd sure appreciate it if you could let me have a little sugar," Pete said slyly.

"I got nothing but lump sugar," Moore retorted.

"That's what I want anyway," Pete said. "It's for my horse. He didn't feel like coming into your camp with me. He seemed to remember not liking it around here much."

"Beat it!" Moore snapped. "If you come around here again, you'll be in trouble. I could easy enough tell the sheriff about that stolen horse you're keeping."

"He's just as much mine as he could be anybody's. I've got a right to him. He was a wild horse and I gentled him. I'm not breaking any law—any more than a fellow who kills mustangs on the dunes just for fun."

Moore's eyes blazed at this. He shouted in fury, "Get out and stay out, I told you!"

Pete turned and went back to Sandy. Then he rode slowly, thoughtfully down toward camp. He had seen something interesting, all right, but if Moore had a jeep it was concealed in the trees somewhere. And Pete felt sure he knew now what had spooked the wild horses so badly before he began his chase. Moore had been murdering mustangs.

CHAPTER SIXTEEN

PETE'S DISCOVERY

"What do you make of it all?" Pete asked, after he had told Hatsy his day's adventures.

"Same thing I make of the wind," Hatsy replied. "I just let it blow. Moore's as nutty as a fruitcake. Probably thinks he's Chief-Rain-in-the-Face out shooting buffalo. Fact is, I've seen swells on a dude ranch playing with those bow and arrow sets but I never thought I'd live to see one of 'em up here. Anyway my idea is we just keep working on our rag rug and leave him alone."

"You don't think he's a rustler then?" Pete said. He felt somewhat disappointed. He had halfway convinced himself that Moore must be a cattle thief of some sort, playing some fancy trick.

"So far as I know, you're the only rustler around here," Hatsy said. "If my back's all right tomorrow, we better ride out where you can get a good chance to give Sandy some calf-roping practice."

The next morning they trotted off west of the dunes in search of likely calves with the Lazy B-5 brand on them. As they rode, Pete kept feeling the short piece of rope he had quietly tucked under his belt. He hadn't asked Hatsy, but he intended not only to rope a calf but to throw it and hogtie it with the short rope, the way the cowhands did at branding time. He'd seen it done in rodeos, and he didn't want Sandy to be the only one who learned something new today.

Sighting a white-faced Hereford cow and her late calf who hadn't yet been weaned, Pete unlimbered his rope and formed a good loop.

The calf didn't take to its heels until they were quite close. Just as Pete let fly with his rope, the little animal dodged like a rabbit at right angles, and the loop didn't even touch him.

Full of delight at racing in the open country, Sandy kept straight on. Pete had the job both of reining him in and recoiling his rope which was snapping around. By the time he had got Sandy turned back and the rope coiled, the calf was a long way off. Pete decided that next time he'd guide Sandy in pursuit of the calf without making any attempt to rope. Sandy had to learn how to chase the dodging, quick little animals first.

Half a dozen times in the next hour he pursued calves without roping. Each time, Sandy seemed more interested in the game. Finally, taking off after a calf, Pete knew that Sandy had really caught on. The calf headed toward the dunes, then zigzagged off to the right, then back toward the dunes. With each sudden break in one direction or the other,

Sandy followed close. This time, Pete decided, he would make a cast. He swung his rope and dropped the loop neatly over the calf's head, and then reined in. But the chase was too much fun for Sandy. He kept running alongside the frightened creature. A wild shake of the calf's head, and it was free. Pete never had a chance to pull the rope taut.

Now Pete was way ahead of Hatsy and decided he'd better wait till the old man caught up. He waved his sombrero to signal he was staying and swung one leg up around the saddlehorn. His eyes traveled idly over the dunes. Along the edge near by something caught his attention. There were rocks lying on the sand—a whole cluster of them, with no other stones near. Pete nudged Sandy over close to them and saw that they were arranged in a definite pattern, as if they had been put there on purpose.

Quickly Pete dismounted and found that some of the stones were just ordinary rocks from the bed of a stream, set in circles. Others were queerly shaped —some were hollowed out, and in the hollows or near by lay rounded stones like rolling pins without handles. Pete came closer and found scattered here and there shiny, sharp-edged arrowheads. No grass grew around the place. Apparently it was usually covered with sand, but now only a little sand remained.

Pete looked around for Hatsy and waved his hat

urgently. These must be old Indian relics, he decided. He began to pick up the arrowheads and fill his sombrero with them.

As Hatsy jogged up, Pete ran with the hat to show what he had found.

"Look at these arrowheads!" he said excitedly. "There's a lot more junk here, too."

Fishing into the sombrero Hatsy fingered one after another of the delicately shaped flint and chert points. He looked closely at the tiny irregularities in the edges, studied, and felt the shapes.

"Looks like these arrowheads were made by either the Utes or Comanches," Hatsy said. "They both hunted in this valley until the Utes finally drove the Comanches out."

He dismounted and walked with Pete over to the place where the larger stones lay. Pete watched him going from stone to stone and felt real pleasure at the old man's interest in what he had discovered.

"Did you move any of this stuff?" Hatsy asked.

"Only this stone here," Pete said, picking up one of the rolling-pin objects.

"Where was it to begin with?" Hatsy asked.

"About here." Pete pointed and then replaced it. "What do you make of it?"

Hatsy ignored the question and kept on, picking up an arrowhead here and there. He scuffed the sand occasionally and twice picked up a stone hatchet or tomahawk head. Finally he paused.

"Looks like a good yarn spinner could tell quite a story about what you've found here, Pete," Hatsy said. "Mainly I'm good at just telling what's as plain as the hand in front of my face. 'Course I can lie like a politician, too. But now I'm not either lying or telling the truth. I just have a dang good idea what must have happened here."

Hatsy picked up one of the rolling-pin rocks and put it into the hollow of one of the large flat stones near by. "See how this fits? Put some corn into the hollow, roll this rock back and forth over it, and you've got cornmeal before long. That's the way the Indians in the pueblos down in New Mexico always made cornmeal—and still do."

"I thought you said the arrowheads were Ute or Comanche," Pete interrupted.

"I did. That's where the story comes in. Nobody but Pueblo Indians ever used these big stones for grinding corn. And Pueblo Indians never lived here, as far as I ever heard. But I know they used to come up here hunting deer and antelope. There were still lots of antelope in the valley when I first hove in. Chances are the Pueblos packed this stuff along and camped here. A lot of Indians thought the dunes were some kind of magic. Maybe those circles of stones had something to do with dances or ceremonies they did."

"The Pueblo Indians Make Cornmeal With This."

Hatsy paused, then went on, "Now it looks like they set up a camp here and then lit out in a hurry. Nobody leaves corn-grinders like that around carelessly. They take a long time to make. This is what I figure must have happened. These Pueblo Indians had been rustling deer and antelope in territory the Utes and Comanches claimed was theirs. On the side, the Pueblos were getting in some of their ceremonials, too. They sure got a lot of them. I've seen 'em. They'd a lot rather dance than fight. They were probably busy carrying on with a big fandango when the rightful owners of the valley dropped in for an unexpected call. Looks like the raiders were mighty poor shots. There are plenty of arrow points around but no bones. If anybody was killed, the coyotes sure made off with them."

Pete had never been so close to Indian things before and he was excited both by his find and by Hatsy's guess as to what had happened. "But that must have been a long time ago," he said. "How come nobody's ever picked all this stuff up?"

"Probably nobody ever saw it from that day to this," Hatsy replied. "Chances are those Pueblos camped here just when a freak wind had cleared the ground of sand. Then after they hightailed out, the ordinary kind of wind blew all the sand back and covered everything up."

"Then another freak wind in the last few days

must have cleared the sand away from the place,"
Pete said.

"And there's no telling how long it will stay
cleared away either," Hatsy replied. "It could be
covered up during the night again. This stuff is
worth collecting. Let's get to work."

Pete picked up one of the big corn-grinding sets
and started to lug it toward the horses.

"That's not what I mean by get to work," Hatsy
said. "We ought to do this right. There's a lot more
here than we can wrap up in our slickers. I'll go get
the wagon and we'll make a real job of it. We'll have
to camp here tonight, because the chances are we
won't get through before dark."

"I better go with you," Pete said. "We can pack
up faster if there are two of us."

When they had finished packing, back at camp,
Hatsy pulled a stub of old pencil out of his war-bag
and found a paper sack from under the wagon seat.
"You take these," he said to Pete, "and ride on ahead
to our Indian place. While you're waiting for me,
you draw a map of the whole thing. I saw some college professors once down in Arizona digging up
old-time Indian things, and this is how they did it.
They put numbers on every piece of stuff. Then
they put the same numbers on a map in the right
places."

"I don't get it," Pete said in surprise.

"I got a suspicion that some museum feller would be interested in what you found," Hatsy said. "You can't put it all in your suitcase and take it back to Chicago, and I'm not going to lug it around forever in my wagon."

"Jeepers, I'd like to keep some of it myself!" Pete exclaimed.

"Time enough to worry about that later," Hatsy said. "Giddap."

As Pete went on ahead at a fast trot, he found himself thinking what a good kind of guy old Hatsy was. Here he was, spending his summer helping a strange tenderfoot get a horse and then knocking himself out to help some museum get a collection of Indian relics. Still, Pete felt, it wouldn't hurt the museum any if a few of the arrowheads ended up in his room in Chicago. He was sure Hatsy would agree to that.

By the time Hatsy reached the Indian find, Pete had completed his map. He had measured the distances in strides and had drawn a little circle on the map for each of the larger rocks, corn-grinders, and hatchets. He hesitated at first about the arrowheads, but they seemed to be lying in no particular pattern. So he picked them up as he found them, for fear they would be scuffed over with sand as he and Hatsy moved about.

Hatsy drove the wagon up close. "How you coming?" he called and climbed down from the seat.

"I've got the map," Pete answered. "What about the numbers?"

"You tether the horses off there where there's some good grass," Hatsy said, pointing, "while I get the hang of this picture of yours."

In ten or fifteen minutes Pete was back.

"We start on this side," Hatsy said. "You hand me a rock. I'll put a number on it and I'll put the same number on the map in the right place. Then you can stow the stuff in the wagon. But not on top of the bedrolls. We're going to need them tonight. When we're through tomorrow we'll let Lem worry about finding a place for our rock pile in his barn."

By the time it was too dark to work, they were well over half finished with the job. Wearily, Pete made a fire, and Hatsy warmed up a quick meal. Then both of them were asleep, almost before they could crawl into their soogans.

CHAPTER SEVENTEEN

DANGER IN THE DUNES

Pete woke with the first gray of dawn the next morning. He dimly realized that something had changed. It had been quiet when he fell asleep, but now there was a snapping and rattling coming from the wagon over his head. Everywhere there seemed to be a loud moan. The wind was blowing and blowing hard.

He was out of his bedroll in an instant and saw that sand was already sifting heavily down over the bedrolls and the remaining Indian relics. The loose end flaps of the canvas wagon cover were whipping in and out crazily.

"Come on," he called to Hatsy who was crawling out of his blankets. "We have to hurry."

After a quick look around, Hatsy said, "You get the team and we'll pull the wagon out of here before the sand piles up to the hubs. Better tie your handkerchief over your nose. While you're gone, I'll see if there's any of those Indian things I can save. The sand'll be piling up like snowdrifts in a hurry. It may be a couple of hundred years before this place ever opens up again, and I'm fresh out of steam shovels."

For the first time Pete appreciated the many uses of the cowboy neckerchief he had been wearing. With it over his nose, he could breathe more easily, although the sand stung his eyes, as he jog-trotted toward the horses. Luckily the place where they were tethered was out of the center of the sandstorm, but it was a real chore to lead the Apaloosas back to the wagon.

"I'm going to hitch up now," Pete called. "Okay?"

No answer came. The wind was too loud for the old man to hear, probably. Pete looked around for him. Hatsy was nowhere to be seen. Holding the horses' lead ropes, Pete lifted the flaps and looked into the wagon. Hatsy wasn't there, either. Pete hopped down and looked through the stinging sand toward the place where the Indian relics had been, then out toward the plain to see if Hatsy might have gone in that direction. There was no sign of him anywhere.

Frightened now, Pete dropped the Apaloosas' lead ropes and began to search. Hatsy had said he'd pick up more stones. He must be close. Squinting, with his eyes almost shut, Pete stumbled across the small area where the Indian camp had been. Suddenly his moccasined feet hit something in the soft sand. It was Hatsy, already partly covered in the creamy-white drift of the dunes. With his back to the wind, Pete knelt down over the old man who lay with one arm thrown over his face. His hat was gone. Shielding Hatsy's head from the wind, Pete frantically pushed the sand away. The thin old body lay there, breathing quietly.

There was only one thing to do and Pete did it. Although he suspected what had happened, he felt Hatsy's legs and arms to make sure the old man hadn't stumbled and broken a bone. Then he grabbed Hatsy beneath the shoulders and dragged him to the rear of the wagon. As gently as he could, he eased Hatsy's spare frame up onto the tailboard. Inside the canvas cover, he would be protected, and in a moment Pete could have the Apaloosas hitched up. Then he could drive away from the dunes and their swirling sand.

Pulling Hatsy in through the back flap, Pete stretched him out on the bedrolls that the old man had tossed in on top of the Indian stones. Now he could harness the Apaloosas who were standing restlessly beside the wagon. As he thrust up the canvas cover to jump out, the wind caught it and made it flap against itself with a report like a rifle. The sharp noise, together with Pete's quick leap to the ground, sent the already nervous horses into a frenzy. Both reared as one, and broke into a frantic race across the sand ahead of the wind. Well-trained though they were, the Apaloosas had been stampeded by the storm.

Pete Dragged Hatsy to the Wagon

Deep inside, Pete felt as if he were almost ready to stampede, too. But with a great effort he forced himself to stop and think. He couldn't move the wagon now. He couldn't tell how long the storm would last or how high the sand would pile up around the wagon—or in it. He didn't dare leave Hatsy there alone long enough to go to the ranch for help. Pete knew what he had to do. He must get Hatsy to the ranch on Sandy. That wouldn't be easy. Sandy might spook at the wind—or at carrying double, which he had never done before. Still, Pete had to take the chance.

He knew that the storm might make Sandy nervous, so he decided he had better saddle him away from the dunes, right where he was tethered. It was a job to lug the forty-pound saddle in the heavy wind, but before long he had it on Sandy's back. Riding toward the wagon, he talked soothingly to the horse: "Sandy, you've got a big job to do—the biggest job you ever had. You and I have to take Hatsy back to the ranch so we can get a doctor."

At the wagon, Pete tied Sandy to the rear wheel. Then he made a pad of a blanket, and lashed it over the saddlehorn. Now he had to bring Hatsy out onto the tailgate and fasten a heavy strap around his chest, under his arms. The old man was still breathing as if he were in a heavy sleep.

Pete planned out every move he was going to make

next. He untied and mounted Sandy, then edged
him up so that he was alongside the tailboard.
Knotting the reins, he dropped them over the saddlehorn and cautiously, using both hands, he
gripped the strap and drew Hatsy across the saddle,
face down.

Sandy shied away from the wagon at the unexpected weight and gave a startled toss of his head
when the canvas cover flapped loudly. But with one
hand on the reins, Pete managed to quiet him. With
an effort, Pete raised the limp body high enough so
he could draw the old man's right leg over the saddlehorn. Now both of them were squeezed into the
saddle. Pete eased himself back over the cantle and
sat astride the saddle-skirt with both feet out of the
stirrups. This would be the test. With the wind sending Sandy's mane streaming forward over his eyes,
and his tail blown between his legs, the horse
strained every muscle to break into a gallop. Pete
held him in firmly, but was careful about pulling too
hard on the bit for fear Sandy would rear and throw
his double burden. At last Sandy settled down, and
headed away from the dunes. Pete kept his right arm
around Hatsy's chest, supporting the limp figure.
With his left hand, he held the reins and gave addi-
tional support.

Before long his arms were aching with the strain.
Pete rested them as best he could by shifting posi-

tion. Once as he shifted, he thought he felt Hatsy stir. Although the wind still blew, it was no longer filled with sand, and the early morning sun began to warm Pete. It shone back from the pale white skin on the top of Hatsy's bobbing head. At that moment Pete realized what must have happened. Something must have struck the sensitive spot on the top of the old man's head when his hat blew off in the storm. Hot sun on the spot wouldn't help any. Holding the whole weight with his left arm, Pete transferred his own sombrero to Hatsy's head. It was much too big, so he held it in place by pulling the chin-strap tight under Hatsy's jaw.

Presently he was aware that Hatsy's head no longer bobbed limply, and he realized that there was much less weight on his arms. "Hatsy!" Pete said anxiously. There was no answer. "Hatsy?"

"Seems kind of crowded around here," came a tired, thin voice. "If you'll quit tickling my ribs, I'll see what I can do about getting my feet in the stirrups."

Pete gave a nervous laugh of pleasure and relief. "You all right?"

"It might be stretching matters a little to say that, until I get the general hang of what's going on. Let loose of me, I said."

Pete dropped his right arm, but held onto the reins with his left hand.

Hatsy reached up and felt the unfamiliar covering on his head. "Where's my hat?" he demanded. "This thing sure is heavy on my ears."

"Maybe we'd better stop and rest awhile," Pete suggested.

"Nothing as restful around here as a saddle, and I'm in it," Hatsy retorted. "What kind of a picnic is this, anyway?"

Pete told about finding him unconscious and almost buried in the sand, about the Apaloosas' being spooked, and about his plan to get Hatsy to the ranch.

Hatsy listened and said finally, "Last thing I remember, I was bent over and reaching up to grab at my hat. Felt like the wind was just about to make off with it. I guess it blew off, all right, and I got hit on my soft spot by a little stick or something that was riding along on the wind. I told you that you could hit me with a feather there and send me plumb loco."

"Are you all right now?" Pete asked again.

"Nothing wrong with me that a new hat won't fix," the old man said. "I'll order that up as soon as we get to the ranch. But it looks like you'll still have a job after that. My Apaloosies would keep right on running if they saw me with this thing on my head. You'll have to go bring them in and get the wagon, too, I guess."

"I guess I should have tied them when I went off looking for you," Pete said. "But I didn't figure how scared they'd be by the racket of that flapping canvas."

"Wouldn't have tied 'em myself," Hatsy answered. "Those horses know when they are supposed to stand. It was a fool thing of me not to lash my hat on tight."

Pete felt relieved. It wasn't his fault that Hatsy had been injured. And he knew that this time he had thought things clear through.

CHAPTER EIGHTEEN

SANDY SPOOKS AGAIN

"Hey, Lem! Hey, Clary!" Hatsy called as they rode up to the ranch house.

Aunt Clara appeared at the kitchen door, wiping her hands on her apron.

"Tell Lem I brought in that rustler that's been after his calves."

Pete grinned as he slid down from his perch behind Hatsy.

"Why, Pete!" Aunt Clara exclaimed. "Whose horse is that? Lem! Lem! What's that on your head, Hatsy?"

"Give me a hand down, Pete," Hatsy said. "My back's been flat broke, Clary, ever since you made me sleep in that bed of yours."

Uncle Lem appeared from the barn. "Been horse-trading, Hatsy?" he drawled.

"This here Chicago gangster just rustled it," Hatsy answered. "He's the same hombre that Pedro saw roping your calves. I'm bringing him in for justice."

"Rubbish, Hatsy!" Aunt Clara said impatiently. "Pete, I won't give you a bite to eat unless you tell straight out what you've been up to."

Pete grinned and helped Hatsy out of the saddle. "I have to water my horse first, Aunt Clara," he said. "Then I'll tell you." Pete emphasized the *my* just a little.

"I never could talk on an empty stomach," Hatsy said. "Breakfast turned up missing this morning, Clary. Maybe you better quit being so high and mighty and fix us a mess of flapjacks."

"Oh, pshaw!" Aunt Clara said and went into the house, while Pete took Sandy to the watering trough.

Still wearing Pete's hat, the old man smacked his lips appreciatively as he finished off a pile of pancakes. Pete hadn't talked either. It was too much fun to wait and see what Hatsy would say or do next.

"Well, now, I'll tell you," Hatsy began. "One day Pete and I were sitting working on our rag rug—"

"Hatsy, I'll never let you in this house again," Aunt Clara broke in. "Quit wasting our time and get down to business."

"There are different ways to tell a story," Hatsy protested.

"I don't want any stories," Aunt Clara snapped.

Hatsy saw it was no use. He'd have to give a report. When he had finished telling how Pete and he had caught and gentled Sandy, and how Pete and Sandy had got him out of the sandstorm, Uncle Lem said with real admiration, "Why, then, Pete, you saved Hatsy's life. He'd have been buried there in the dunes along with the Indian stuff if you hadn't used your head just when you did."

Pete was both pleased and embarrassed.

"Speaking of heads," Hatsy said, "I gotta get something to cover mine."

"I'll drive you in to the store in Alamosa," Uncle Lem offered.

"I never wore a store hat in my life," Hatsy snorted. "I always get mine through the mail from John B. Stetson himself in Philadelphia. You ought to know that. How do you think I'd look in one of those dude-ranch things?"

"It's the best we can do right now," Aunt Clara put in. "You've got to have a hat and it'll take a time to get your kind through the mail. You can just wear a store one for a while, till John B. gets around to sending one of his."

"I guess that's right," Hatsy admitted. "But if I act kind of poorly for a while, you'll know why. I can't take any strength and energy from a store hat."

Now it was agreed that Pete should ride Sandy back, find the Apaloosas, and bring in the wagon. He was sure he wouldn't need any help. The horses, if they had run far at all, had probably gone back to the familiar camp at the box canyon. In any case, they wouldn't wander far.

"You needn't expect me till sometime tomorrow," Pete said. "I'll go to the wagon first and get a bedroll, just in case."

His aunt and uncle and Hatsy came out to see him off. Pete couldn't resist riding Sandy around in the yard to show how well he performed. If they noticed the horse's big feet, they didn't mention them. They were much too pleased with Pete and what he had done.

On the way back to the dunes, Pete wanted nothing more in the world than to let Sandy cover the ground at a triumphant gallop. But he decided he'd better save his mount's strength. There was no telling how much work lay ahead.

The windstorm had ended. When Pete reached the wagon he saw the sand had piled up about a foot around the wheels. And sand had sifted into the wagon bed, covering everything there inches deep. He dug out his bedroll, shook it, took some cans of food from the chuck box, and headed off north in the direction in which he had last seen the Apaloosas.

By the time he reached the mouth of the canyon, he had seen no signs of them. Nor were they at the box canyon. Pete decided the best thing would be to ride to the place where he had first sighted the mustangs—a high, open spot from which he had a wonderful view on three sides. From there he might be able to see Raindrop and Polkadot.

He followed along behind the dunes for quite a way before turning up the slope of the mountain. It

Pete Found Sand Piled Around the Wagon

had been a hard day for Sandy, but he still climbed with spirit. When they were high enough for a good view, Pete dismounted to let Sandy rest and graze for a little while. He looked across the great waste of the dunes below him searching for the Apaloosas out on the flats. He saw cattle, but no horses. Maybe he'd have a lot of riding to do tomorrow. Raindrop and Polkadot must have kept going to the north.

Pete was about to stretch out for a rest when he caught sight of something in the sand at the edge of the dunes below him. He looked more sharply. In spite of the distance, he thought he could make out the outlines of a jeep, and near it was something dark in the sand. He remembered Hatsy, half-buried that morning. Could it be the driver of the jeep who had had an accident of some kind? Even if it were Moore, Pete couldn't just go away. He felt he ought to investigate.

He zigzagged down the mountainside as fast as he could. Soon he could see that his guess had been correct about one thing at least. It was a jeep, all right, with sand drifted high around it. As a precaution, Pete tied Sandy to an aspen close to the dunes, and hurried toward the jeep on foot. There was no one in it. But the dark object near by was not a man. Pete dismounted and looked in amazement. There at his feet were the neatly severed heads of two deer —one a doe and one a buck—and a heap of offal, undoubtedly the insides of the same animals. The drifting, unpredictable sand that might have buried the heap entirely had left it partly exposed.

A lot of things began to add up suddenly in Pete's mind. He stepped over to the jeep for a closer look. In the rear end was a washtub, drifted half-full of sand. It was bloody and had obviously been used to carry the deer parts.

Pulling the sand away with his hands, he found the jeep's Colorado license plate and memorized the number. Then he brushed the sand off the seat and tipped it up to see what he could find. There he saw some tools and a letter which had apparently slipped down behind the seat. It was addressed simply to Leonard Moore—no postage stamp, no address— and it came from the Ashmore Hotel in Colorado Springs.

Shamelessly, Pete opened it and read:

Dear Mr. Moore: The last delivery of chickens was received and payment has been credited to your account. The beef, however, was spoiled on arrival and had to be rejected. You will have to be more careful about refrigeration in the future.

"It looks as if Moore's in the wholesale meat business, when he isn't out camping," Pete thought to himself. Then, "Wait a minute!"

It could be that Moore was rustling beef—and poaching, too. All signs pointed toward Moore as far as the dead deer were concerned. If the guy was shooting does, it wasn't hard to understand why Pete had seen the little fawns running around alone. But what was he doing out here on the dunes with the jeep? Pete supposed it was just easier to bury refuse in the sand than in the hard earth on the mountain. He remembered how neat Moore's camp was. And he supposed the jeep had been abandoned in the big sandstorm that morning.

Suddenly Pete realized he'd better leave. Moore might return any minute to dig the jeep out, and Pete had no desire to be caught prying into the man's private affairs. Besides he wanted to find the Apaloosas and hurry back to the ranch with his story of the jeep.

He tossed the letter down and put the seat back into place over it. The ceaseless wind which shifted the sand was already concealing the fact that he'd been there by the time Pete mounted Sandy and rode off.

The sun was dropping behind the San Juan mountains as Pete reached the place where he and Hatsy had first camped. He would spend the night here. It was even possible that the Apaloosas might come to the creek there for water in the morning and save him the trouble of hunting further. If he didn't find them by the next evening, he'd go back to the ranch to see whether the cowhands had any trace of them.

Next morning, Pete was wakened by a sharp whinny from Sandy. Answering whinnies came from near by. His hunch about the Apaloosas had been very lucky indeed. There were Raindrop and Polka-dot trotting down to the creek for water.

CHAPTER NINETEEN

When Pete rattled up to the ranch in the wagon, leading Sandy behind, Hatsy came out of the house wearing a new sombrero. Aunt Clara and Uncle Lem appeared, called hello, and went back to their chores. Pete knew they were busy and he'd have a chance to talk with them later.

As he and Hatsy unharnessed the team and turned the horses into the pasture, Pete told of his new discovery about Moore. He was, in fact, a little relieved that his aunt and uncle weren't hearing this part of the story right now. He didn't want to worry them, and he felt sure he and Hatsy could handle whatever might come up.

"Looks like a certain deputy game warden had better stick to game-wardening and not let any more Indians get him off the trail," Hatsy said.

"What do you think we ought to do?" Pete asked.

"Now I gotta admit there's an advantage to autos," Hatsy said. "They have to wear number plates. We'll phone up the government first and find out who made the mistake of giving a license to that jeep. After that we'll think some more."

Pete wrote down the number he had memorized

from the license plate, and Hatsy went into the house. A minute or two later Uncle Lem and Aunt Clara came out.

"Hatsy says you found a dingus for making cornmeal," Aunt Clara told Pete. "What's he talking about this time?"

Pete guessed that Hatsy wanted to be alone to make the telephone call. He jumped up into the wagon and fished out one of the Indian corn-grinders. "Look," he said. "The Indians used it like this." He demonstrated the roller in the hollow stone.

"I get my cornmeal easier from the store," Aunt Clara said flatly. "I have enough work without that."

Pete was afraid that she might go back into the house. "That's not all. Look at what else we found." He pulled out some axes, more corn-grinders, and handfuls of arrowheads.

"Seems like you must have run into where there was a massacree," Aunt Clara said, a little more interested.

Pete jumped at this and told them Hatsy's story of what probably had happened at the Indian camp. Hatsy sauntered out of the house as Pete was finishing the story.

"Pete," Hatsy said, "seeing I'm deputy game warden, I have to go out tomorrow and depute a little. Want to come along?"

"Sure," Pete said, forgetting that his aunt and

uncle might be worried about his going off into some kind of trouble.

"I thought you wanted to ride fence," Uncle Lem said. "You've got a horse now that looks like he could do it."

"If you need me, I'll stay," Pete answered.

"We'll make out for a couple of days all right," Uncle Lem said, smiling.

"Are you two in your right minds?" Aunt Clara protested. "You just got out of a big mess. Don't look for any more trouble."

"I haven't got as old as I am by looking for trouble," Hatsy said. "We'll only be gone three or four days, touring around some country Pete's not seen before. Then I'm through with you folks. I'm going to take myself up to my old stamping grounds, where the scenery isn't crowded with anything but trout."

"I suppose you know what you're doing," Aunt Clara said reluctantly.

Uncle Lem agreed to let Pete store the Indian relics in canned-goods cartons on the floor in the grain room of the barn. Pete unloaded the stone things, and then Hatsy supervised packing the wagon with a new food supply which Aunt Clara let them have.

"We don't need too much this time. We can get more where we're going," Hatsy said to Pete.

"Where's that?" Pete asked.

"Time enough to talk things over after we get started," Hatsy answered.

"I'm not Aunt Clara," Pete said. "You don't have to keep secrets from me. Give. What about the jeep license?"

"Government feller said it belonged to a man by the name of Moore in Colorado Springs," Hatsy said.

"All right," Pete said. "Here's the way it seems to me. I don't know what you've figured out, but I do know what I think would make good sense."

Then he told Hatsy a theory and a plan for action he had been building up in his own mind.

First of all, Moore must be selling illegal meat in Colorado Springs. The letter showed that. Second, he must have a helper, because he couldn't get the meat *and* drive it to Colorado Springs himself. That would take too much time. Third, he must have a regular route that he traveled and a place where his helper picked up the meat.

Pete didn't know the valley well, but he knew only one main road led from their part of the valley over the mountains to Colorado Springs. That was the one Pete had traveled when he came in from Chicago —the LaVeta Pass road.

Either Moore's helper came in from this road to his camp, or Moore brought the meat out and met the helper somewhere on the road.

Since a jeep could travel almost anywhere, it seemed more likely that Moore brought the meat out of the hills and met his helper.

Therefore, all they had to do was find the meeting place and catch the two crooks with the goods.

"The only thing that bothers me," Pete finished, "is this. We oughtn't to waste time. Moore may have got suspicious and cleared out by now, even."

"That's the only place you're wrong," Hatsy said. "As far as Moore is concerned, we are the ones who skipped out. We've left our camp—gone off with the horses and the wagon. He thinks we're through bothering him. He may even think he scared us off. He came up here with big plans for a whole summer, and he'll think he's got less reason than ever to be worried. Chances are your tracks around his jeep were sifted over with sand before he got back. He won't suspect a thing."

"We still haven't answered another question, either," Pete said. "How are we going to locate the place where Moore meets his helper? It would be hard to trail him without being seen."

"I kind of figure a couple of tourists with a wagon and an extra horse may pick up the answer to that along the LaVeta Pass road," Hatsy answered. "In fact, if I was Moore, I know just where I'd come out on that road. It would be a place that would give me a good hot meal without me being too conspicuous.

There's a certain diner, name of *Custer's Last Stand,*
over that way. It's the only place in miles where
truck drivers can get good coffee and pie. Old man
Custer is used to having regular truck-driver customers. And he don't ask unpopular questions,
either. So Moore would feel safe going there."

Pete thought back over his trip in to the ranch.
He didn't remember seeing the diner, but he knew it
must be a good long way off. It turned out that he
was right. At the easy pace Hatsy set, they were two
days crossing the flat valley floor, and it was dark on
the second day before they drew near the main road
which led gently up toward the Pass.

Both days Pete had ridden Sandy, only occasionally tying his horse to the tail of the wagon and sitting
down beside Hatsy to keep the old man company.
He had discovered that Sandy had a wonderful natural canter—a pace that made Pete feel as if he were
riding in a rocking chair. And Sandy never seemed
to get tired. Even Hatsy said it had been a long time
since he had seen a horse with such endurance.

Instead of traveling the last couple of miles on the
highway, which they might have done, Hatsy guided
the Apaloosas along parallel with it.

"I'm aiming to pull up into a grove of trees just
this side of Custer's place. The less fuss about it the
better," he said.

The darkness was broken by the headlights of cars

now and then, speeding along the highway, and Pete
could soon see the glow from the diner.

"We'll turn in here," Hatsy said.

The place they were approaching was a thick
grove of trees which Hatsy said Custer had planted,
hoping to develop a picnic spot and improve his
trade. Nothing much had come of his scheme, and
he had let the underbrush grow. A couple of hundred yards beyond stood the diner with a few shade
trees behind it and gasoline pumps near the highway
in front.

"We'll have to get water for the horses at the
diner," Hatsy said. "There hasn't been any here, except in Custer's well, since Noah climbed out of the
Ark."

Pete helped unhitch the Apaloosas, but did not
wait to unsaddle Sandy. Leading all three horses,
they picked their way through the trees. Toward the
middle of the grove, Hatsy called in a low voice,
"Hold up a minute and keep quiet." After a pause,
he added, "There's a truck here."

Pete stopped. He had almost bumped into the rear
end of a van which had been backed off the road in
among the trees.

Hatsy dropped the Apaloosas' lead ropes and
stepped cautiously to the front of the van to see if
anyone was in it. No one was there. Suddenly he
struck a match close to the rear doors. Sandy shied

"There's a Truck Here, Pete."

and almost pulled the reins out of Pete's hand. "Hey, watch it, Hatsy," Pete said in a low voice. At the same moment he saw by the matchlight that water was dripping out from under the doors of the van, which were closed but not padlocked.

"Let me hold Sandy," Hatsy said. "You climb in the back of this truck and have a look around. I got a feeling it's our business to see why it's backed in here all by its lonesome."

Pete opened one of the van doors and clambered inside. Striking a match, he said, "Nothing in here but some crates of lettuce and some big cakes of ice. Seems like a lot of ice for such a small load."

"Okay, hop down and close her up. Let's see what we can find out behind here," Hatsy said. "I'll bet you can locate jeep tracks around close."

Lighting a match now and then, Pete examined the ground close by. There, sure enough, were the narrow tracks made by a jeep. He followed them a little way and found that he could trace a beaten-down road through the underbrush. It headed off at right angles to the main highway.

"Just like we figured," Hatsy said. "Here's the end of Moore's trail. He drives up through these trees, so as not to be noticed too much. Unless I'm crazy the guy who drives the truck is in the diner now waiting for Moore. Let's go."

As they approached the diner, the bright lights

and the roar of a passing truck startled Sandy again. "Take all the horses around to the back of the diner," Hatsy said to Pete.

"Sandy won't be bothered so much by the lights at least if he's back there. I'll go in and borrow some water from Custer and have a look around."

Waiting in the darkness behind the building, Pete got more and more restless. Hatsy seemed to be taking a long time. The horses needed water and Pete realized all at once that he was hungry. No cars had passed, and Sandy had been quiet. Then Sandy gave a nervous shuffle of his feet and snapped his head up attentively. There was nothing on the highway, coming from either direction.

But as Pete turned to give his horse a reassuring pat, he saw what had been disturbing Sandy. A flicker of moving lights shone through the trees. They were approaching the highway from the barren plains to the north. This must be Moore in the jeep.

CHAPTER TWENTY

WRAPPED IN CELLOPHANE

Where was Hatsy? Moore was driving up into the grove now, and for all Pete knew Hatsy had started telling one of his long stories to Custer. Pete didn't dare leave the horses. He had an impulse to call out, but stopped himself in time. Then he heard footsteps. Hatsy came around the end of the diner, sloshing a pail of water in each hand.

"Look!" Pete said in a low voice. "There in the grove. It's Moore."

"Good! I got Custer all set inside. I looked through the window and saw the feller that drove Moore to the ranch in the jeep. No other customers. So I sneaked in through the pump shed and gave Custer the high sign to come out. He said another feller that seemed to look like Moore came in here regular about this time of night."

The two Apaloosas were noisily drinking from the buckets. Sandy would have to wait till the next round.

"I'll tell you what," Pete said. "Moore will probably come up here. As soon as he does, I'll sneak over and have a look at the jeep. There's nothing we can do unless he's got something with him that he shouldn't have."

Pete had been keeping his eye on the grove. Now he heard footsteps approaching, and soon was able to pick out the dim silhouette of a man. Was it Moore? Sandy gave the answer. He snorted and tugged at his reins. At the sound of the horse, which he couldn't see in the darkness behind the diner, the man paused. Then, apparently deciding there was nothing to investigate, he kept on, and in the light from the diner Pete saw Moore's bulky figure and city hat.

When the diner door had slammed, Hatsy said, "I'll tie the Apaloosies here and wait around outside. After you've looked at the jeep, go over to the wagon and get out my war-bag. There's an old six-shooter in it. It looks wicked enough and might come in handy."

Pete swung into the saddle and turned Sandy toward the grove. When he reached the trees, the horse grew more and more nervous. Pete guessed that it was still Moore's scent that upset the horse. Dismounting at the edge of the grove he tied Sandy to a tree, then pushed through the brush toward the place where they had found the truck. Feeling his way, he reached the truck first. Parked a few feet behind it he found the jeep.

Pete lit a match. The back of the jeep held a large, canvas-covered object. Working by feel, he untied a corner of the canvas which was damp. Under it was a big metal container, very cold to the touch. He threw the canvas back still farther, then felt around in the dark and found a movable lid which he raised with one hand while he reached inside with the other.

His fingers closed first around a small chunk of ice. Probing further, they grasped something cool and soft and slippery. Puzzled, he lit another match and looked into the box. The small, flickering flame revealed Cellophane-wrapped packages surrounded by chunks of ice. Pete lifted out a package to examine it more carefully. Through the transparent wrappings, he could see a duck with its feathers still on. Pete felt certain that if he examined the duck he'd find it had been caught with a fish hook and not shot. He put it back and reached in again. This time he found a wrapped chunk of something that could only be meat.

Pete dropped the lid and was just pulling the canvas back down when he heard Hatsy's thin sharp voice shouting, "Pete, Pete! Watch it! Watch it!"

Pete scrambled through the brush toward Sandy. Against the light of the diner, he saw a figure—it could only be Moore—running toward the grove. Sandy was dancing nervously as Pete untied the reins and swung into the saddle.

Almost without thinking, Pete turned the horse

toward the running figure. Hearing the commotion ahead, Moore hesitated, started to swerve, stumbled, and fell flat. He was on his feet again in an instant, but, apparently confused, ran toward the highway. That was all Pete needed to see. He touched Sandy with his boot heels and the horse bounded forward obediently.

The next moment Pete had his rope uncoiled and was shaping a loop. With the man between him and the light of the diner, he could see well enough to make a cast. In the dim glow, the rope sailed out and fell over Moore's shoulders. Reining in Sandy and pulling the rope taut at the same instant, Pete jerked the man off his feet. Moore's arms were pinioned to his sides at the elbows.

"Hatsy!" Pete yelled. "I got him."

"I'm coming," the old man called.

Moore tried to scramble to his feet. But Pete touched Sandy again and jerked the man flat on his back, dragging him a little way before he could stop the horse. Now Hatsy was close enough to see what had happened. The fall had dazed Moore, but he tried again to get up. With just a sharp pull of the rope, Pete kept him off his feet.

"Lie still, Moore," Hatsy ordered. "I'll scalp you with this milk bottle I got in my hand if you make a move. And Pete can drag you around this way till the sheriff comes, if you ain't peaceable."

Moore said nothing and lay staring up. Pete managed to keep Sandy fairly quiet, but every once in a while he shied a little, giving a sharp tug to the taut rope.

"What did you find, Pete?" Hatsy asked.

"A lot of ducks and meat," Pete answered.

"Okay, Moore, we got the goods on you," Hatsy said. "For your information, I'm a game warden. Your partner's in the diner looking at the business end of Custer's Colt. Now I'll tell you what you're going to do, and don't try any funny business till I finish. I'm right here with this milk bottle. You're going to roll over, and keep rolling over, toward the horse, till I say stop. Pete, you give him just enough slack on the rope so he can wrap himself up in it. Ready now. Roll."

Moore didn't stir for a moment, and Pete was afraid he would make a sudden move, loosen the loop, and try to get away.

But Hatsy flourished the milk bottle over the man's head. "Want Pete to drag you in? Get rolling," he ordered.

With an angry growl, Moore heaved himself over and began to wind himself in the rope. When there were four turns of it pinning his arms tight to his body, Hatsy said, "Now get on your knees and bend over."

Handing Pete the milk bottle, Hatsy took the end

of the rope and knotted it firmly behind Moore's back.

"All right, Moore. Get up and don't look around. Now walk slow to the diner."

Clumsily Moore heaved himself onto his feet and obeyed. Pete had his hands full managing Sandy as they came closer to the brightly lighted front of the diner. Moore kept edging away from the horse and seemed relieved to step in through the doorway at last.

"Got another customer for you," Hatsy called out, as he shoved Moore down toward the end of the diner where the truck driver stood with his hands over his head.

Pete was reluctant to miss anything, but he couldn't leave Sandy here. Quickly he tied him near the quiet Apaloosas at the back of the diner, then ran around to the front entrance.

"Give us a hand, Pete," Hatsy said. Moore and the truck driver were standing in the corner of the diner, and Custer was leaning over the counter with his heavy old Colt pointed at them. "Custer says he's got some clothesline out in his pump shed. Go through the door behind the counter and see if you can rustle it up."

Pete found the clothesline in a hurry and brought it back.

"Now, you hombres," Hatsy said, "we could play

'hands up' from now till the law comes for you. But that would kind of interfere with Pete and me getting a bite to eat, which we came here for. So we're going to let you sit down nice and comfy at the counter. Moore, you're first. Come over and fork this stool."

Moore didn't move.

"Maybe you didn't hear right," Hatsy said. "I said sit on this stool."

Custer waggled his gun and Moore went to the stool as he had been ordered.

"Now, Pete, you lash his feet to the footrest down there so he won't get bucked off."

Pete had a vision of getting kicked in the head, but with a few swift turns of the rope he had Moore tied so he couldn't leave the stool which was fixed to the floor. The other man came next, still with his hands in the air. Pete lashed his feet and then bound his hands behind him.

Hatsy inspected the knots, and said at last, "I'll call the law now." When he had finished his call, he swung up beside Pete who was sitting on a stool at the counter.

Custer grinned and said, "What'll it be, gents? It's on the house."

"Ham and eggs and apple pie a-la-mode," Pete said promptly. He had been looking at the blackboard with the menu chalked on it all the time

Hatsy was phoning.

"Wait a minute," Hatsy said. "What did you find in that jeep, Pete?"

"Ducks and meat, wrapped up fancy and packed in ice," he said.

Hatsy considered a minute. "It's a little late to start roasting a duck. But the meat might be kind of interesting. Pete, you borrow Custer's flashlight and get us a sample."

When Pete returned with a large chunk of meat, Hatsy and Custer examined it carefully before removing the Cellophane. "It's wrapped as purty as a box of chocolates," Hatsy said. "Except there's no ribbon on it. I saw chickens done up this way once in a fancy store in Tucson. But I never heard of anybody camping out on a mountainside and going to all that trouble." He took off the wrapping and studied the meat. "Custer, write venison steak on your menu. I'm cooking it. It's your night off. You sit here like a paying guest, picking your teeth with that old shooting iron of yours."

Pete had never tasted venison, and he was eager to try it, but he wondered a little whether they would be breaking the law to eat it. "What'll the sheriff say?" he asked.

"He'll say he has to confiscate the meat and give it to a hospital or a poorhouse or something. But the law won't begrudge us a little reward we hand ourselves for stopping a rattlesnake that'll kill does and ducks out of season."

While Pete went out to water and unsaddle Sandy, Hatsy got to work.

CHAPTER TWENTY-ONE

TWENTY-DOLLAR QUESTIONS

Hatsy slapped three plates on the counter with a flourish. Pete leaned over and sniffed the dark, wonderful-smelling meat in front of him. The first bite surprised him. It was different from what he had expected—very rich-tasting and a little sweet. It was good, though, and he was hungry. But he couldn't see why anyone would risk going to jail in order to get it.

After they had polished off their plates in silence, Hatsy said, "Custer, this drugstore cowboy is going to feel starved unless he gets apple pie and ice cream. I don't know where you hide it, so you better take over."

As Custer dished up dessert for the three of them, he said, "How about telling me exactly what this little rumpus is all about?"

"If Moore would give us some help, we could spin you a pretty good yarn," Hatsy replied. "Pete, you tell him what you know."

Moore and the driver had been sitting perfectly quiet. Neither of them showed any interest now. Pete told Custer about Moore's arrival at the ranch and about seeing him later around their camp. He told of finding the signs of duck poaching, of the motherless fawns and the mustangs that had been killed. He described Moore's camp and his skill with the bow and arrow.

At that point, a huge trailer truck pulled up in front of the diner, and the driver came in. He whistled when he saw the two captives lashed to the stools. "What you doing, Custer? Sticking up tourists? Aren't you satisfied with the prices you already hold 'em up for?"

Custer explained briefly and then asked Pete to go on. Pete began again and told of finding the jeep in the sand and the letter from the hotel in Colorado Springs.

"I know that joint," the trailer-truck driver interrupted. "It's a place for swells—the kind that think money can buy anything. Must be they get a special kick out of eating stuff that ordinary people can't have."

"Well, now, I've figured out something," Hatsy exclaimed, addressing Moore. "First I thought maybe you were a rustler. But then I couldn't see how your runt-sized stink wagon could haul enough of any kind of meat to be worth your while. You must have been getting a mighty fancy price for every pound of that stuff you shipped out."

For the first time, Moore started to say something, then shut up. An impish look came onto Hatsy's face. He said to Custer, "Waiter, fix Mr. Moore and his friend a glass of your best water—with a straw, please. He'll pay for it at your regular rates." With that Hatsy pulled a wallet out of Moore's back pocket, looked into it, and whistled. "It's kind of hard to find anything as small as a one-dollar bill here." But he pulled out two and gave them to Custer with great ceremony. Custer produced the water, with straws in the glasses, and laid the bills under his gun on the counter.

Hatsy was obviously getting warmed up with an idea. He took all the money out of the wallet and laid it in a pile on the counter. "Mr. Moore," he said acting like an auctioneer at a country sale, "I know you are anxious to turn a quick penny. Here is a chance. This twenty-dollar bill is yours if you will explain to my friends here what you were doing with a bow and arrow."

Moore moved uncomfortably on his perch. Still he didn't say anything.

Hatsy looked around with a broad wink. "The question is now open to anybody, that includes Mr. Moore's friend, too. I don't think we've been introduced." Gently, he pulled a wallet from the hip pocket of Moore's helper. Taking out the driver's license, Hatsy said, "Folks, meet Mr. Harry Foster. Well, now, Hank, it doesn't seem you're so well fixed. Less than ten dollars here. Maybe you'd like to

answer that question I just asked for twenty dol·
lars."

Before Foster could even splutter, the trailer-truck
driver put in, "I got an answer, and I could sure use
twenty dollars. Your friend was playing cupid with
his bow and arrow."

"Best I've heard so far," Hatsy said, and he handed
the bill to the driver, who slipped it under his coffee cup.

Pete had been perplexed at the beginning of this
performance, but now he was laughing inside, fit to
bust. He knew Hatsy. Moore's money was perfectly
safe. But Moore already looked as if he might begin
to talk.

Pete politely shoved Hatsy aside and picked up
another twenty-dollar bill. "Gentlemen," he said,
"this money goes to anyone who can tell me why Mr.
Moore wraps his meat up fancy like Christmas
packages?"

"That's easy," Custer said. "Meat keeps better
that way. You can throw ice all around it and it
won't get wet when it's wrapped up tight. Water
spoils meat."

Pete handed him the bill. Custer put it with the
others under his gun.

Moore burst out at last, "Give a guy a break.
That's my money."

"You mean it's yours if you answer the questions

Pete Was Laughing Inside, Fit to Bust

right," Hatsy said amiably. "The law ought to be here in about half an hour. You better hurry up and talk. The money goes to the man with the best answers."

Moore snorted, but said nothing else.

After a moment, Hatsy said, "This twenty dollars goes to anyone who tells why Mr. Moore, Mr. Leonard Moore, shot mustangs with his bow and arrow."

Pete almost shouted, "Because he's just naturally mean and likes to kill things."

"*Forty* dollars for that answer," Hatsy chuckled, and handed over the bills.

Moore turned his eyes quickly from Pete. "That's a lie," he said. "I'd had plenty of practice on a target, but I needed practice on running animals if I was going to get enough deer out of the place to make it pay."

Hatsy peeled off two more bills. "You've tied for that answer, Mr. Moore," he said. "Forty dollars to you, too. Maybe you'd like to bid on some of those other questions. You can have the whole pile if you come clean."

Everyone was silent. Hatsy riffled the bills like a deck of cards on the counter. Then he looked around. "You fellows got any questions?"

"How do I know you'll give me my money?" Moore asked shrewdly.

"Tell you what I'll do," Hatsy replied. "I'll put it

back in your wallet and into your pocket right now. As long as you keep talking, it stays there. But if you don't speak up sensible, there's others that have good answers ready."

Moore was sweating by now. But he seemed to figure that he had a lot to lose if he didn't talk—and something to gain if he did. So he told his story. Pete wanted to catch every word. He heaved himself up so that he could sit on the counter, with his feet on the stool, and leaned toward Moore. Some of the things he heard he'd already expected. Others were news.

Moore used to be a butcher in a town not far north of New York City. Then he lost his job in the meat shop and got another as caretaker on one of the large estates near by. Some of the country around there in Westchester County was wooded, and even so close to the big city there were deer. But the county law said they couldn't be hunted with guns. You could only shoot them with bow and arrow but only during a hunting season. Some people, including Moore's boss, got very skillful at this kind of hunting, and they actually managed to bring down a deer every now and then.

Moore's boss was gone much of the time. When he was away Moore practiced with the bow and arrow. One day, when he was practicing in an open pasture, he saw a deer and shot it. It was his bad luck to be caught. The season was over. Moore was fined for poaching, and his boss fired him, too. He finally wound up in Colorado Springs, with a job as meat-cutter in the Ashmore Hotel. There he discovered that the hotel secretly bought game out of season. Of course, they didn't put it on the menu. The head-waiter just whispered to special customers when they had it. Moore happened to find out how much the hotel paid for ducks and grouse and deer, so he decided he could make a lot more money poaching than he could cutting meat. And he'd do it in a real businesslike way.

First, he found out from Harry Foster where there was a good place for hunting. Harry delivered lettuce to the hotel, every few days in his own truck. He was willing to deliver meat, too, now and then. So they went to work.

At first, Moore concentrated on catching ducks with fishing lines, while he practiced up on his archery. The mustangs made good moving targets. Soon, however, he got his skill back, and was packing a deer into his camp every day or so on the burro. On some of his trips he had run across the horse trap and had broken the line fence.

Then the burro got sick and died. He tried to get another pack animal—first at the ranch, then by stealing Sandy. Also he wanted to make Pete and Hatsy move away because he hated to run the risk of being discovered. Moore knew his main danger came from being seen. His noiseless arrows, of course, were much better weapons than a gun, the sound of which could easily have given him away to anyone passing by.

Moore had taken every precaution against leaving evidence of poaching around his camp. He kept his butchering tools locked in a chest. After cutting up the deer on the table in his extra tent, he washed everything clean, carried away all the waste in the jeep, and buried it in the sand. He kept the jeep hidden among some overhanging rocks a quarter of a mile from his camp. After he got the telltale letter from the hotel about refrigerating his meat, he hauled in an icebox, and every time he brought a load of meat to Foster, he took back a load of ice which Foster got for him.

Nobody lived within miles of the route he followed along the foothills above the dunes. Except for Pete and Hatsy he hadn't seen a soul in all the time he'd been up there. Since Custer wasn't an inquisitive type, Moore and Foster had begun to meet inside the diner freely.

"Now," Moore concluded, "you've got your story. How about giving me a break? You can divide half the money in my pocket if you let me escape before the law comes."

"Still trying to be a cheapskate," Hatsy jeered.

"Half the money!"

"Well—all of it. Just let me out of here," Moore growled desperately.

"That only takes care of you," Hatsy said. "What about your friend Foster here?"

For the first time Foster spoke. He was furious with Moore. "Yeah, what about me?"

"Maybe he'll give you his truck," Moore said, sneeringly.

"For a smart city slicker he don't learn very fast," Hatsy said scornfully, turning to the others. "He just opened up the jail doors good and wide for himself by trying to bribe an officer of the law. You fellers were witnesses."

Still sitting on the counter, Pete saw headlights approaching on the highway. "Somebody's coming," he said. "Game's over—team's goin' home."

He hopped down, gathered up all of the money that was lying on the counter, and stuffed it in Moore's pocket along with his purse. Hatsy replaced the wallet in Foster's pocket, too.

Then he peered through the window as the car stopped in front of the diner and three men got out. "Yep, looks like we don't have to wait any longer," Hatsy said.

A tall, youngish officer pushed open the diner door. "Howdy," he said. "Fellow here who goes by the name of Hatsy?"

"That's me," Hatsy said. "And this here is Chicago Pete, the new cowpoke at Lem Perkins's place. He's responsible for catching the two coyotes you came out here for."

CHAPTER TWENTY-TWO

SANDY'S CHOICE

Sandy was frisky—a tawny skin full of life. He pranced under the trees in Custer's grove as Pete threw the Navaho saddle blanket on his back. The horse was obviously enjoying the crisp early morning air. As for Pete, every morning that he saddled Sandy gave him a thrill of pleasure. But today he felt special delight. The pony was as fresh as if he hadn't been traveling steadily for two days. It seemed almost as if he were showing off for Hatsy as a kind of farewell salute.

Today would be Pete's and Sandy's last with the old man—for a while, at least. Hatsy was packing the supplies he'd got from Custer and readying his wagon for the fishing trip into the Sangre de Cristos that he had postponed while Sandy was being gentled.

Through the trees, Pete saw the poacher's van waiting to be taken away. One of the officers had driven off last night in the jeep with its load of evidence. Pete chuckled again at the way in which Hatsy had out-talked the officers, convincing them that he could have his vacation instead of hanging around the court to tell the judge these men were poachers. Anybody could see that, he argued.

Now the old man climbed into the wagon seat and clucked to his team. Pete mounted, and they started off, following Moore's jeep trail. Once out of the trees, Pete galloped on ahead, letting Sandy work off his excess steam. In a minute he pulled up to wait for the wagon. But there it was, just about where he had left it. Beside it in the sagebrush stood an automobile.

Pete's heart sank. Would they have to go to the court after all? He trotted back toward the wagon.

"Feller here wants to see you," Hatsy called. As Pete pulled up, he added, "Says he's from the newspaper, and he wants to meet up with Chicago Pete. I already told him a few things."

Pete was pleased and embarrassed, too. He dismounted and answered the young reporter's questions, which seemed to cover almost everything, starting with when he was born.

"Do you mind if I take a picture of you, too?" the reporter asked at last.

"I guess not," Pete answered self-consciously.

"Stand over here," the reporter said, motioning him out into the open.

"Not just me," Pete said. "You have to take Sandy, too." He moved over to the pony.

"Sure," Hatsy said. "That's a genu-wine sand dune mustang. Pete caught him and gentled him himself. You could write about that, too, and about the time Pete and his pony saved my life."

But Pete's protest meant nothing. Hatsy insisted on telling the whole story of the sandstorm and the Indian relics. When the reporter had found out everything he seemed to want, he thanked Pete and Hatsy and said good-by.

"Wait a minute, partner," Hatsy said. "I just thought of something. You can do Pete a favor if you want to. You might just call up some perfessor feller at the college in Alamosa and ask him to pick up that Indian stuff for a museum. It's sitting in the barn at the Lazy B-5—unless Clary Perkins has heaved it out because of the clutter it makes. Pete will be back at the ranch by tomorrow night, and he can tell the perfessor a lot I bet he doesn't know."

Agreeing to deliver the message, the reporter took a final picture of Pete as he swung into the saddle beside the wagon.

Now they moved steadily along the sloping foothills, following Moore's jeep trail. Hatsy was going to continue all the way up to Moore's camp. Then he would push on to his secret fishing grounds high above. At the dunes, Pete would leave the old man and head for the ranch. He was eager to get some work with Uncle Lem's cowhands, before he had to go back to school in Chicago.

It was well into the afternoon when they reached

the place where they planned to separate. Pete checked the bedroll and the food that he had tied at the back of the saddle. Then he shook hands with Hatsy and started to say a quick thanks for everything.

"The best way to thank me is to make sure Clary doesn't throw out my new Stetson when it comes," Hatsy said. "Tell her I'll be down to pick it up before the leaves start turning. Adios, partner." He flipped the reins, and the Apaloosas turned the wagon up the trail behind the dunes.

Pete watched till the strange-looking outfit had disappeared behind the first ridge. Then he headed Sandy toward the dunes. "You might as well have one last run here in your old home before you start being a full-time cow pony," he said.

Near the south end of the dunes there was a point at which the sandy waste narrowed. Pete planned to cut across here, out onto the alkali flats, then turn north toward the ranch.

As the horse felt the sand under his feet once more, Pete sensed a little change in his gait which helped him keep a sure footing. It seemed to Pete there was always something new to find out about Sandy. When they were well up into the dunes, Sandy paused and pricked up his ears, sniffing with nostrils alert and sensitive. Pete felt that the horse was interested, not afraid. He let Sandy have his head.

Sandy turned up a ridge and trotted along as if with real purpose. Then, with a whinny, he sped up. Pete saw why.

On a ridge to the west, stood a small band of the wild mustangs—the old stallion at their head. Startled now, the band raced down behind the ridge and disappeared. Sandy slowed his pace, and after a moment shook his head, as if waiting for Pete to give him direction.

Pete had been tense with excitement and doubt. Would Sandy try to rejoin the band? But now he knew. Sandy had left the dunes forever. He had chosen between the wild band and Pete.

The whole valley and its magnificent rim of mountains stretched out ahead for them to explore —together.